ABOUT THE AUTHOR

MICHEL HOUELLEBECQ is a French novelist, poet, and literary critic. His novels include the international bestseller *The Elementary Particles* and *The Map and the Territory*, which won the 2010 Prix Goncourt. He lives in France.

ABOUT THE TRANSLATOR

LORIN STEIN is the editor of *The Paris Review*. He lives in New York.

ALSO BY MICHEL HOUELLEBECQ

FICTION

Whatever

The Elementary Particles

Platform

The Possibility of an Island

The Map and the Territory

NONFICTION

H. P. Lovecraft: Against the World, Against Life

*Public Enemies: Dueling Writers Take On
Each Other and the World*
(with Bernard-Henri Lévy)

Additional Praise for *Submission*

"The political elements of *Submission* are so comically exaggerated that it's hard to take them very seriously. . . . This is the novel's big joke. It's designed to agitate the right by suggesting the right may have a point about the erosion of France's national culture, and to tweak the left by lending ironic credence to the right's fears. . . . The only time Houellebecq seems not to be joking is when Francois speaks about literature. . . . Whatever it says or doesn't say about Europe and Islam, *Submission* is a love letter to the novel itself."
—Christian Lorentzen, *New York* magazine

"Houellebecq's recent work—especially *The Map and the Territory*, one of the finest novels of the twenty-first century—is elegant, sad, all the more discomfiting in that we never quite know how much subtlety to credit the author with. Houellebecq writes on shifting sands, but I think he might just be permanent."
—Michael Robbins, *Chicago Tribune*

"Extraordinary . . . If there is anyone in literature today, not just in French but worldwide, who is thinking about the sort of enormous shifts we all feel are happening, it's [Houellebecq]."
—Emmanuel Carrère, *Le Monde*

"Houellebecq has an unerring, Balzacian flair for detail, and his novels provide an acute, disenchanted anatomy of French middle-class life. . . . Houellebecq writes about Islam with curiosity, fascination, even a hint of envy."
—Adam Shatz, *London Review of Books*

"A work of real literary distinction . . . [Houellebecq] has been the novelist who has most fearlessly and presciently tackled the rise of Islamic extremism in recent years. . . . He is a writer with a gift for telling the truth, unlike any other in our time—I've been consistently saying he is the writer who matters most to me for many years now. I've read *Submission* twice in the last week with ever-growing admiration and enjoyment. There's been no English-language novel this good lately. With *Submission*, Houellebecq has inserted himself right into the center of the intellectual debate that was already raging in France about Islam and identity politics. . . . There is nobody else writing now more worth reading."

—David Sexton, *London Evening Standard*

"Michel Houellebecq: butcher. Messy slaughterer of sacred cows. Disembowler of all modes of political correctness, from the myth of the modern male's respect for women to the laughable fiction of the liberal Westerner's respect for non-Western cultures. That's the story, anyway. Like most good stories, it isn't true; for the most part . . . [*Submission*] is a work of genius, sure—with Houellebecq, that goes without saying. But it's not a slaughterhouse. It's an upper-middle-class supermarket, brightly but not harshly lit, stocked with sushi, expensive cheeses, organic vegetables, olive oils, and honeys. It's not food for thought. It's an empty stomach. It's heartbreaking. It's utopia."

—Micaela Morrissette, *BOMB*

"The prose, which never fails to be consistent and accessible, continued to impress page after page. . . . Perhaps the highest achievement of [*Submission*] is the way it manages to be a satire with a core of deep humanism running through it."

—*Popmatters*

"Houellebecq's deadpan comedic edge . . . defies the reader to find the line between parody and philosophy. . . . What Houellebecq has done in *Submission* is hold up a mirror to his readers. The charge is that he inflames animosity by depicting a Muslim-influenced France as something of which Europeans should be frightened. But he puts readers and critics in the position of having to specify what exactly is frightening about this France."

—S. Mark Heim, *The Christian Century*

"[*Submission*'s] moral complexity, concerned above all with how politics shape—or annihilate—personal ethics, is singular and brilliant. . . . This novel is not a paranoid political fantasy; it merely contains one. Houellebecq's argument becomes an investigation of the content of ideology, and he has written an indispensable, serious book that returns a long-eroded sense of consequence, immediacy, and force to contemporary literature."

—*Publishers Weekly* (starred review)

"It would be easy to object to [*Submission*] based on hearsay alone, but Houellebecq is both too skillful as a novelist to be saying anything merely polemical, and far too intelligent to ignore."

—Gaby Wood, *The Telegraph* (London)

SUBMISSION

Michel Houellebecq

TRANSLATED FROM THE FRENCH BY LORIN STEIN

Picador

Farrar, Straus and Giroux

New York

SUBMISSION. Copyright © 2015 by Michel Houellebecq and Flammarion. Translation copyright © 2015 by Lorin Stein. All rights reserved. Printed in the United States of America. For information, address Picador, 175 Fifth Avenue, New York, N.Y. 10010.

picadorusa.com • picadorbookroom.tumblr.com
twitter.com/picadorusa • facebook.com/picadorusa

Picador® is a U.S. registered trademark and is used by Macmillan Publishing Group, LLC, under license from Pan Books Limited.

For book club information, please visit facebook.com/picadorbookclub or e-mail marketing@picadorusa.com.

The translator wishes to acknowledge the good counsel of Antonin Baudry, Paul Elie, Stephen Andrew Hiltner, Violaine Huisman, Mark Lilla, John McGhee, Marco Roth, Sadie Stein, John Jeremiah Sullivan, and especially his editor, Mitzi Angel. Any errors remaining are his own.

The Library of Congress has cataloged the Farrar, Straus and Giroux edition as follows:

Houellebecq, Michel, author.
    Submission / Michel Houellebecq ; translated from the French by Lorin Stein.—First American edition.
        p. cm.
    ISBN 978-0-374-27157-2 (hardcover)
    ISBN 978-0-374-71448-2 (e-book)
    1. Religions—Relations—Fiction. 2. Political campaigns—France—Fiction. 3. Political corruption—France—Fiction. 4. Political campaigns. 5. Political corruption. 6. Religions—Relations. 7. France. I. Title.
    PQ2668.O77 S6813 2015
    843'.914—dc23   2015949676

Picador Paperback ISBN 978-1-250-09734-7

Our books may be purchased in bulk for promotional, educational, or business use. Please contact your local bookseller or the Macmillan Corporate and Premium Sales Department at 1-800-221-7945, extension 5442, or by e-mail at MacmillanSpecialMarkets@macmillan.com.

Originally published in France as *Soumission* by Flammarion

First published in the United States by Farrar, Straus and Giroux

First Picador Edition: November 2016

10 9 8 7 6

I

A noise recalled him to Saint-Sulpice; the choir was leaving; the church was about to close. "I should have tried to pray," he thought. "It would have been better than sitting here in the empty church, dreaming in my chair—but pray? I have no desire to pray. I am haunted by Catholicism, intoxicated by its atmosphere of incense and candle wax. I hover on its outskirts, moved to tears by its prayers, touched to the very marrow by its psalms and chants. I am revolted with my life, I am sick of myself, but so far from changing my ways! And yet . . . and yet . . . however troubled I am in these chapels, as soon as I leave them I become unmoved and dry. In the end," he told himself, as he rose and followed the last ones out, shepherded by the Swiss guard, "in the end, my heart is hardened and smoked dry by dissipation. I am good for nothing." —J.-K. Huysmans, *En route*

Through all the years of my sad youth Huysmans remained a companion, a faithful friend; never once did I doubt him, never once was I tempted to drop him or take up another subject; then, one afternoon in June 2007, after waiting and putting it off as long as I could, even slightly longer than was allowed, I defended my dissertation, "Joris-Karl Huysmans: Out of the Tunnel," before the jury of the University of Paris IV–Sorbonne. The next morning (or maybe that evening, I don't remember: I spent the night of my defense alone and very drunk) I realized that part of my life, probably the best part, was behind me.

So it goes, in the remaining Western social democracies, when you finish your studies, but most students don't notice right away because they're hypnotized by the desire for money or, if they're more primitive, by the desire for consumer goods (though these cases of acute product-addiction are unusual: the mature, thoughtful majority develop a fascination with that "tireless Proteus," money itself). Above all they're hypnotized by the desire to make their mark, to carve out an enviable social position in a world that they believe and indeed hope will be competitive, galvanized as they are by the worship of fleeting icons: athletes, fashion or Web designers, movie stars, and models.

For various psychological reasons that I have neither the skill nor the desire to analyze, I wasn't that way at all. On April 1, 1866, at the age of eighteen, Joris-Karl Huysmans began his career as a low-ranking civil servant in the French Ministry of the Interior and Ecclesiastical Affairs. In 1874 he published, at his own expense, a first collection of prose poems, *Le drageoir à épices*. It received next to no attention, apart from one extremely warm review by Théodore de Banville. Such were his quiet beginnings.

His life as a bureaucrat went on, and so did the rest of his life. On September 3, 1893, he received the Légion d'Honneur for public service. In 1898 he retired, having completed—once leaves of absence were taken into account—his mandatory thirty years of employment. In that time he had managed to write books that made me consider him a friend more than a hundred years later. Much, maybe too much, has been written about literature. (I know better than anyone; I'm an expert in the field.) Yet the special thing about literature, the *major art form* of a Western civilization now ending before our very eyes, is not hard to define. Like literature, music can overwhelm you with sudden emotion, can move you to absolute sorrow or ecstasy; like literature, painting has the power to astonish, and to make you see the world through fresh eyes. But only literature can put you in touch with another human spirit, as a whole, with all its weaknesses and grandeurs, its limitations, its pettinesses, its obsessions, its beliefs; with whatever it finds moving, interesting, exciting, or repugnant. Only literature can grant you access to a spirit from beyond the grave—a more direct, more complete, deeper access than you'd have in conversation with a friend. Even in our deepest, most lasting friendships, we never speak so openly as when we face a blank page and address an unknown reader. The beauty of an author's style, the music of his sentences, have their importance in literature, of course; the depth of an author's reflections, the originality of his thought, certainly can't be overlooked; but an author is above all a human being, present in his books, and whether he writes very well or very badly hardly matters—as long as he gets the books written and is, indeed, present in them. (It's strange that something so simple, so seemingly universal, should actually be so rare, and that this rarity, so easily observed, should receive so little attention from philosophers in any discipline: for in principle human beings possess, if not the same quality, at least the same quantity, of being; in principle they are all more or less equally *present*; and yet this is not the impression they give, at a distance of several centuries, and all too often, as we turn pages that seem to have been dictated more by the spirit of the age than by an individual, we watch these wavering, ever more ghostly, anonymous beings dissolve before our eyes.) In the same way, to love a book is, above all, to love its author: we wish to meet him again, we wish to spend our days with him. During the seven years it took me to write my dissertation, I got to live with Huysmans, in his more or less permanent presence. Born in the rue Suger, having lived in the rue de

Sèvres and the rue Monsieur, Huysmans died in the rue Saint-Placide and was buried in Montparnasse. He spent almost his entire life within the boundaries of the Sixth Arrondissement of Paris, just as he spent his professional life, thirty years and more, in the Ministry of the Interior and Ecclesiastical Affairs. I, too, lived in the Sixth Arrondissement, in a damp, cold, utterly cheerless room—the windows overlooked a tiny courtyard, practically a well. When I got up in the morning, I had to turn on the light. I was poor, and if I'd been given one of those polls that are always trying to "take the pulse of the under-25s," I would certainly have checked the box marked "struggling." And yet the morning after I defended my dissertation (or maybe that same night), my first feeling was that I had lost something priceless, something I'd never get back: my freedom. For several years, the last vestiges of a dying welfare state (scholarships, student discounts, health care, mediocre but cheap meals in the student cafeteria) had allowed me to spend my waking hours the way I chose: in the easy intellectual company of a friend. As André Breton pointed out, Huysmans's sense of humor is uniquely generous. He lets the reader stay one step ahead of him, inviting us to laugh at him, and his overly plaintive, awful, or ludicrous descriptions, even before he laughs at himself. No one could have appreciated that generosity more than I did, as I received my rations of celery remoulade and cod puree, each in its little compartment of the metal hospital tray issued by the Bullier student cafeteria (whose unfortunate patrons clearly had nowhere else to go, and had obviously been kicked out of all the acceptable student cafeterias, but who still had their student IDs—you couldn't take away their student IDs), and

I thought of Huysmans's epithets—the *woebegone* cheese, the *grievous* sole—and imagined what he might make of those metal cells, which he'd never known, and I felt a little bit less unhappy, a little bit less alone, in the Bullier student cafeteria.

But that was all over now. My entire youth was over. Soon (very soon), I would have to see about entering the workforce. The prospect left me cold.

The academic study of literature leads basically nowhere, as we all know, unless you happen to be an especially gifted student, in which case it prepares you for a career teaching the academic study of literature—it is, in other words, a rather farcical system that exists solely to replicate itself and yet manages to fail more than 95 percent of the time. Still, it's harmless, and can even have a certain marginal value. A young woman applying for a sales job at Céline or Hermès should naturally attend to her appearance above all; but a degree in literature can constitute a secondary asset, since it guarantees the employer, in the absence of any useful skills, a certain intellectual agility that could lead to professional development—besides which, literature has always carried positive connotations in the world of luxury goods.

For my part, I knew I was one of those "gifted" few. I'd written a good dissertation and I expected an honorable mention. Yet to my surprise I received a *special commendation*, and I was even more surprised when I saw the committee's report, which was excellent, practically dithyrambic. Suddenly a tenured position as a senior lecturer was within my reach, if I wanted it. Which meant that my boring, predictable life continued to resemble Huysmans's a century and a half before. I had begun my adult life at a university and would probably end it the same way, maybe even at the same one (though in fact this wasn't quite the case: I had taken my degree at the University of Paris IV–Sorbonne and was hired by Paris III, slightly less prestigious but also in the Fifth Arrondissement, right around the corner).

I'd never felt the slightest vocation for teaching—and my fifteen years as a teacher had only confirmed that initial lack of vocation. What little private tutoring I'd done, to raise my standard of living, soon convinced me that the transmission of knowledge was generally impossible, the variance of intelligence extreme, and that nothing could undo or even mitigate this basic inequality. Worse, maybe, I didn't like young people and never had, even when I might have been numbered among them. Being young implied, it seemed to me, a certain enthusiasm for life, or else a certain defiance, accompanied in either case by a vague sense of superiority toward the generation that one had been called on to replace. I'd never had those sorts of feelings. I did have some friends when I was young—or, more precisely, there were other students with whom I could contemplate having coffee or a beer between classes and not feel disgust. Mostly I had mistresses—or rather, as people said then (and maybe still do), I had *girlfriends*, roughly one a year. These relationships followed a fairly regular pattern. They would start at the beginning of the school year, with a seminar, an exchange of class notes, or what have you—one of the many social occasions, so common in student life, that disappear when we enter the workforce, plunging most of us into a solitude as stupefying as it is radical. The relationship would take its course as the year went by. Nights were spent at one person's place or the other's (in fact, I'd usually stay at theirs, since the grim, not to say insalubrious, atmosphere at mine hardly lent itself to *romantic interludes*); sexual acts took place (to what I like to think was our mutual satisfaction). When we came back from summer vacation and the school year began again, the relationship would end, almost always at the girl's initiative. *Things had changed* over the summer. This was the reason they'd give, usually without elaboration. A few, clearly less eager to spare me, would explain that they had *met someone*. Yeah, and so? Wasn't I *someone*, too? In hindsight, these factual accounts strike me as insufficient. I don't doubt that they had indeed met someone; but what made them lend so much weight to this encounter—enough to end our relationship and involve them in a new one—was merely the application of a powerful but unspoken model of amorous behavior, a model all the more powerful because it remained unspoken.

The way things were supposed to work (and I have no reason to think much has changed), young people, after a brief period of sexual vagabondage in their very early teens, were expected to settle down in exclusive, strictly monogamous relationships involving activities (outings, weekends, vacations) that were not only sexual, but social. Yet there was nothing final about these relationships. Instead, they were thought of as apprenticeships—in a sense, as *intern-*

ships (a practice that was generally seen in the professional world as a step toward one's first job). Relationships of variable duration (a year being, according to my own observations, an acceptable amount of time) and of variable number (an average of ten to twenty might be considered a reasonable estimate) were supposed to succeed one another until they ended, like an apotheosis, with the last relationship, this one conjugal and definitive, which would lead, via the begetting of children, to the formation of a family.

The complete idiocy of this model became plain to me only much later—rather recently, in fact—when I happened to see Aurélie and then, a few weeks later, Sandra. (But if it had been Chloé or Violaine, I'm convinced I would have reached the same conclusion.) The moment I walked into the Basque restaurant where Aurélie was meeting me for dinner, I knew I was in for a grim evening. Despite the two bottles of white Irouléguy that I drank almost entirely by myself, I found it harder and harder, and after a while almost impossible, to keep up a reasonable level of friendly conversation. For reasons I didn't entirely understand, it suddenly seemed tactless, almost unthinkable, to talk about the old days. As for the present, it was clear that Aurélie had never managed to form a long-term relationship, that casual sex filled her with growing disgust, that her personal life was headed for complete and utter disaster. There were various signs that she'd tried to settle down, at least once, and had never recovered from her failure. The sourness and bitterness with which she talked about her male colleagues (in the end we'd been reduced to discussing her professional life: she was head of communications for an association of Bordeaux winemakers, so she traveled a lot to promote French wines, mainly in Asia) made it painfully clear that she had been *through the wringer*. Even so, I was surprised when, just as she was about to get out of the taxi, she invited me up "for a nightcap." She's really hit rock bottom, I thought. From the moment the elevator doors shut, I knew nothing was going to happen. I didn't even want to see her naked, I'd rather have avoided it, and yet it came to pass, and only confirmed what I'd already imagined. Her emotions may have been through the wringer, but her body had been damaged beyond repair. Her buttocks and breasts were no more than sacks of emaciated flesh, shrunken, flabby, and pendulous. She could no longer—she could never again—be considered an object of desire.

My meal with Sandra followed a similar pattern, albeit with small variations (seafood restaurant, job with a pharmaceutical CEO), and it ended much the same way, except it seemed to me that Sandra, who was plumper and jollier than Aurélie, hadn't let herself go to the same degree. She was sad, very sad, and I knew her sorrow would overwhelm her in the end; like Aurélie, she was nothing but a bird in an oil slick; but she had retained, if I can put it this way, a superior ability to flap her wings. In one or two years she would give up any last matrimonial ambitions, her imperfectly extinguished sensuality would lead her to seek out the company of young men, she would become what we used to call a *cougar*, and no doubt she'd go on this way for several years, ten at the most, before the sagging of her flesh became prohibitive, and condemned her to a lasting solitude.

•

In my twenties, when I got hard-ons all the time, some-times for no good reason, as though in a vacuum, I might have gone for someone like her. It would have been more satisfying, and paid better, than my tutorials. Back then I think I could have *performed*, but now of course it was to-tally out of the question, since my erections were rarer and less dependable and required bodies that were firm, supple, and flawless.

My own sex life, during my early years as a lecturer at Paris III, hadn't evolved in any notable way. Year after year, I kept sleeping with students, and the fact that we were now teacher and student didn't change things much at all. At the beginning, there was scarcely any age difference between us. Only gradually did an element of transgres-sion enter in, and this had more to do with my rising aca-demic status than with my age, real or apparent. In short, I benefited from that basic inequality between men, whose erotic potential diminishes very slowly as they age, and women, for whom the collapse comes with shocking bru-tality from one year, or even one month, to the next. The one real change, since my student years, was that now I was usually the one who broke it off when the school year began. It wasn't that I was a Don Juan, or yearned for some kind of untrammeled sexual freedom. Unlike my colleague Steve, who also taught nineteenth-century literature to the first- and second-year students, I didn't spend the first days of school eagerly checking out the "new talent." (With his sweatshirts, his Converse, and his vaguely Californian looks, he always reminded me of Thierry Lhermitte in *Les bronzés*, emerging from his cabana every week to assess the new crop at the resort.) If I broke up with these girls, it was more out of a sense of discouragement, of lassitude: I just didn't feel up to maintaining a relationship, and I didn't want to disappoint them or lead them on. Then over the course of the academic year I'd change my mind, owing to factors that were external and incidental—generally, a short skirt.

Then that stopped, too. I'd left Myriam at the end of September, now it was already mid-April, the academic year was coming to an end, and still I hadn't replaced her. Although I had been made a full professor, and so had reached a sort of end point in my academic career, I didn't think the two facts were connected. By contrast, it was just after things ended with Myriam that I saw Aurélie, and Sandra, and there I did feel a connection—a disturbing, unpleasant, uncomfortable connection. Because as I looked back over the years, I had to admit that my exes and I were much closer than we realized. Our episodic sexual relations, pursued with no hope of any lasting attachment, had left us similarly disillusioned. Unlike them, I had no one to talk to about these things, since intimacy isn't something men talk about. They may talk about politics, literature, stocks, or sports, depending on the man, but about their love lives they keep silent, even to their dying breath.

Had I fallen prey, in middle age, to a kind of andropause? It wouldn't have surprised me. To find out for sure I decided to spend my evenings on YouPorn, which over the years had grown into a sort of porn encyclopedia. The results were immediate and extremely reassuring. YouPorn catered to the fantasies of normal men all over the world, and within minutes it became clear that I was an utterly normal man. I knew not to take this for granted. After all, I'd devoted years of my life to the study of a man who was often considered a kind of *Decadent*, whose sexuality was therefore not entirely clear. At any rate, the experiment put my mind at rest. Some of the videos were superb (shot by a crew from Los Angeles, complete with a lighting designer, cameramen, and cinematographer), some were wretched but "vintage" (German amateurs), and all were based on the same few crowd-pleasing scenarios. In one of the most common, some man (young? old? both versions existed) had been foolish enough to let his penis drift off inside his briefs or shorts. Two young women, of varying race, would alert him to the oversight and, this accomplished, would stop at nothing until they liberated his organ from its temporary abode. They'd coax it out with the sluttiest kind of badinage, all in a spirit of friendship and feminine complicity. The penis would pass from one mouth to the other, tongues crossing paths like restless flocks of swallows in the somber skies above the Seine-et-Marne when they prepare to leave Europe for their winter migration. The man, destroyed at the moment of his assumption, would utter a few weak words: appallingly weak in the French films (*"Oh putain!" "Oh putain je jouis!"*: more or less what you'd expect from a nation of regicides), more beautiful and intense from those true believers the Americans ("Oh my God!" "Oh Jesus Christ!"), like an injunction not to neglect God's gifts (blow jobs, roast chicken). At any rate I got a hard-on, too, sitting in front of my twenty-seven-inch iMac, and all was well.

Once I was made a professor, my reduced course load meant I could get all my teaching done on Wednesdays. From eight to ten, I had Nineteenth-Century Literature with the second-years, while Steve taught the same class to the first-years in the lecture hall next door. From eleven to one, I taught an upper-level class on the Decadents and Symbolists. Then, from three to six, I led a seminar where I answered questions from the doctoral students.

I liked to catch the metro a little after seven, pretending I was one of the "early risers" of France, the workers and tradesmen. I was the only one who enjoyed this fantasy, clearly, because when I gave my lecture, at eight, the hall was almost completely empty except for a small knot of chillingly serious Chinese women who rarely spoke to one another, let alone anyone else. The moment they walked in, they turned on their smartphones so they could record my entire lecture. This didn't stop them from taking notes in their large spiral notebooks. They never interrupted, they never asked any questions, and the two hours were over before I knew it. Coming out of class I'd see Steve, who would have had a similar showing, only in his case the Chinese students were replaced by veiled North Africans, all just as serious and inscrutable. He'd almost always invite me for a drink—usually mint tea in the Paris Mosque, a few blocks from school. I didn't like mint tea, or the Paris Mosque, and I didn't much like Steve, but still I went. I think he was grateful for my company, because he wasn't really respected by his colleagues. In fact, it was an open question how he'd been named a senior lecturer when he'd never published in an important journal, or even a minor one, and when all he'd written was a vague dissertation on Rimbaud, a *bogus topic* if ever there was one, as Marie-Françoise Tanneur had explained to me. She was another colleague, an authority on Balzac. Millions of dissertations were written on Rimbaud, in every university in France, the francophone countries, and beyond. Rimbaud was the world's most beaten-to-death subject, with the possible exception of Flaubert, so all a person had to do was look for two or three old dissertations from provincial universities and basically mix them together. Who could check? No one had the resources or the desire to sift through hundreds of millions of turgid, overwritten pages on the *voyant* by a bunch of academic drones. The advancement of Steve's career at the university, according to Marie-Françoise, was due entirely to the fact that he was *eating Big Delouze's pussy.* This seemed possible, albeit surprising. With her broad shoulders, her gray crew cut, and her courses in "gender studies," Chantal Delouze, the president of Paris III, had always struck me as a dyed-in-the-wool lesbian, but I could have been wrong, or maybe she bore a hatred toward men that expressed itself in fantasies of domination. Maybe forcing Steve, with his pretty, vapid little face and his long silken curls, to kneel down between her big thighs brought her to new and hitherto unknown heights of ecstasy. True or false, I couldn't get the image out of my head that morning, on the terrace of the tearoom of the Paris Mosque, as I watched him suck on his repulsive apple-scented hookah.

As usual, his conversation revolved around academic hirings and promotions. I never heard him willingly talk about anything else. That morning he was nattering on about a new hire, a twenty-five-year-old lecturer who'd done his dissertation on Léon Bloy and who, according to Steve, had "nativist connections." I lit a cigarette, playing for time as I tried to think why Steve would give a fuck. For a moment I thought his inner *man of the left* had been roused, then I reasoned with myself: his inner man of the left was fast asleep, and nothing less than a political shift in the leadership of the French university system could ever rouse him. It must be a sign, he said, especially since they just promoted Amar Rezki, who worked on early twentieth-century anti-Semitic writers. Plus, he insisted, the Conference of University Presidents had recently joined a boycott against academic exchanges with Israeli scholars, which had begun with a group of English universities . . .

As he turned his attention to his hookah, which had gotten stopped up, I stole a glance at my watch. It was only ten thirty, I could hardly pretend to be late for my next class. Then a topic of conversation occurred to me: lately there had been more talk about a project, first proposed four or five years ago, to create a replica of the Sorbonne in Dubai (or was it Bahrain? Qatar? I always got them mixed up). Oxford had a similar plan in the works. Clearly the antiquity of our two universities had caught some petromonarch's eye. If the project went through, there'd be real financial opportunities for a young lecturer like Steve. Had he considered throwing his hat into the ring with a little anti-Zionist agitation? And did he think there might be anything in it for me?

I shot Steve a probing glance. The kid wasn't very bright, he was easy to rattle, and this had the desired effect. "As a Bloy scholar," he stammered, "you must know a lot about this nativist, anti-Semitic, um . . ." I sighed, exhausted. Bloy wasn't an anti-Semite, and I wasn't a Bloy scholar. Bloy had come up, naturally, in the course of my research on Huysmans, and I'd compared their use of language in my one published work, *Vertigos of Coining*—no doubt the summit of my intellectual achievements. At any rate, it had gotten good notices in *Poetics* and *Romanticism*, and probably accounted for my being made a professor. In fact, many of the strange words used by Huysmans were not coinages but rare borrowings, specific to certain trades or regional dialects. My thesis was that Huysmans never stopped being a Naturalist, that he took pains to incorporate the real speech of ordinary people into his work, and that, in a sense, he remained the same socialist who had attended Zola's soirées in Medan as a young man. Even as he grew to despise the left, he maintained his old aversion to capitalism, money, and anything having to do with bourgeois values. He was the very epitome of a *Christian Naturalist*, whereas Bloy, desperate for commercial and social success, used his incessant neologisms to call attention to himself, to set himself up as a persecuted spiritual luminary misunderstood by the common run of men. Having assumed the role of mystico-elitist in the literary world of his day, Bloy never stopped marveling at his own failure, or at the indifference with which society, quite reasonably, greeted his imprecations. He was, Huysmans wrote, "an unfortunate man, whose pride is truly diabolical and whose hatred knows no bounds." From the beginning Bloy struck me as the prototype of the *bad Catholic*, who never actually exalts in his faith and zeal unless he's convinced that the people around him are going to hell. And yet when I wrote my dissertation I'd been in touch with various left-wing Catholic-royalist circles who worshipped Bloy and Bernanos, and who were always trying to interest me in some manuscript letter or other, until I realized they had nothing to offer, absolutely nothing—no document that I couldn't easily find for myself in the normal collections.

"You're definitely onto something . . . Reread Drumont," I told Steve, just to make him happy, and he gazed at me with the obedient, naïve eyes of an opportunistic child. When I reached my classroom—today I planned to discuss Jean Lorrain—there were three guys in their twenties, two of them Arab, one of them black, standing in the doorway. They weren't armed, at the moment. They stood there calmly. Nothing about them was overtly menacing. All the same, they were blocking the entrance. I needed to say something. I stopped and faced them. They had to be under orders to avoid provocation and to treat the teachers with respect. At least I hoped so.

"I'm a professor here. My class is about to start," I said in a firm tone, addressing the group. It was the black guy who answered, with a broad smile: "No problem, monsieur, we're just here to visit our sisters . . . ," and he tilted his head reassuringly toward the classroom. The only sisters he could mean were two North African girls seated together in the back left row, both in black burkas, their eyes protected by mesh. They looked pretty irreproachable to me. "Well, there you have them," I said, with bonhomie. Then I insisted: "Now you can go." "No problem, monsieur," he said, with an even broader smile, then he turned on his heel, followed by the other two, neither of whom had said a word. He took three steps, then turned again. "Peace be with you, monsieur," he said with a small bow. "That went well," I told myself, closing the classroom door. "This time, anyway." I don't know just what I'd expected. Supposedly, teachers had been attacked in Mulhouse, Strasbourg, Aix-Marseille, and Saint-Denis, but I had never met a colleague who'd been attacked, and I didn't believe the rumors. According to Steve, an agreement had been struck between the young Salafists and the administration. All of a sudden, two years ago, the hoodlums and dealers had all vanished from the neighborhood. Supposedly that was the proof. Had this agreement included a clause banning Jewish organizations from campus? Again, there was nothing to substantiate the rumor, but the fact was that, as of last fall, the Jewish Students Union had no representatives on any Paris campus, while the youth division of the Muslim Brotherhood had opened new branches, here and there, across the city.

21

On my way out of class (what did those two virgins in burkas care about that revolting queen, that self-proclaimed *analist*, Jean Lorrain? did their fathers realize what they were reading in the name of literature?), I bumped into Marie-Françoise, who proposed lunch. Clearly, it was going to be a social day.

I liked the old bag. She was funny, she was an insatiable gossip, and she'd been at the university long enough, and spent enough time on the right committees, to have better information than anyone would ever entrust to the likes of Steve. She led us to a Moroccan restaurant in the rue Monge. Clearly, it would be a halal day, too.

She got going as soon as the waiter brought our food. Big Delouze was on the way out. The National Council of Universities had been in session since June, and it looked as though they'd choose Robert Rediger to replace her.

Glancing down into my lamb-and-artichoke tagine, I raised my eyebrows. "I know," she said. "It's huge. And it's not just talk—I have it on good authority."

I excused myself, and in the men's room I slipped out my smartphone. You really can find anything on the Internet nowadays. A two-minute search revealed that Robert Rediger was famously pro-Palestinian, and that he'd helped orchestrate the boycott against the Israelis. I washed my hands thoroughly and went back to the table.

My heart sank: my tagine was already getting cold. "Won't they wait for the elections?" I asked, after I'd had a bite. This struck me as a sensible question.

"The elections? The *elections*? What have the elections got to do with it?" Not so sensible after all, I guessed.

"Oh, I don't know. It's just, in three weeks we might have a new president . . ."

"Please, that's all settled. It will be just like 2017, the National Front will make it into the runoffs and the left will be voted back in. I don't see why the council should fart around waiting for the elections."

"But there's the Muslim Brotherhood. They're an unknown quantity. If they got twenty percent, it would be a symbolic benchmark, and could change the balance of power . . ." I was talking utter bullshit, of course. Ninety-nine percent of the Muslim Brotherhood would throw their votes to the Socialists. In any case, it wouldn't affect the results at all, but that phrase *the balance of power* always sounds impressive in conversation, as if you'd been reading Clausewitz and Sun Tzu. I was also rather pleased with *symbolic benchmark*. In any case, Marie-Françoise nodded as if I'd just expressed an idea, and she launched into a long disquisition on the possible consequences, for the university leadership, if the Muslim Brotherhood was voted in. Her combinatory intelligence was fully engaged, but I wasn't really listening anymore. I watched the hypotheses flicker across her sharp old features. You have to take an interest in something in life, I told myself. I wondered what could interest me, now that I was finished with love. I could take a course in wine tasting, maybe, or start collecting model airplanes.

•

My afternoon seminar was exhausting. Doctoral students tended to be exhausting. For them it was all just starting to mean something, and for me nothing mattered except which Indian dinner I'd microwave (Chicken Biryani? Chicken Tikka Masala? Chicken Rogan Josh?) while I watched the political talk shows on France 2.

That night the National Front candidate was on. She proclaimed her love of France ("But which France?" asked a center-left pundit, lamely), and I wondered whether my love life was really and truly over. I couldn't make up my mind. I spent much of the evening trying to decide whether to call Myriam. I had a feeling she wasn't seeing anyone new. I'd run into her a few times at the university and she had given me a look that one might describe as intense, but the truth was she always looked intense, even when she was choosing a conditioner. I couldn't get my hopes up. Maybe I should have gotten into politics. If you were a political activist, election season brought moments of intensity, whichever side you were on, and meanwhile here I was, inarguably withering away.

"Happy are those who are satisfied by life, who amuse themselves, who are content." So begins the article Maupassant published in *Gil Blas* on *À rebours*. In general, literary history has been hard on Naturalism. Huysmans was celebrated for having thrown off its yoke, and yet Maupassant's article is much deeper and more sensitive than the article by Bloy that appeared at the same time in *Le Chat Noir*. Even Zola's objections make sense, on rereading: it is true that, psychologically, Jean des Esseintes remains unchanged from the first page to the last; that nothing happens, or can happen, in the book; that it has, in a sense, no plot. It is also true that there was no way for Huysmans to take *À rebours* any further than he did. His masterpiece was a dead end—but isn't that true of any masterpiece? After a book like that, Huysmans had no choice but to part ways with Naturalism. This is all that Zola notices. Maupassant, the greater artist, grasped that it was a masterpiece. I laid out these ideas in a short article for the *Journal of Nineteenth-Century Studies*, which, for the several days it took me to write it, was much more engaging than the electoral campaign, but did nothing to keep me from thinking about Myriam.

She must have made a ravishing little goth as a teenager, not so long ago, and she had grown into a very classy young woman, with her bobbed black hair, her very white skin, and her dark eyes. Classy, but quietly sexy. And she more than lived up to her promise of discreet sexuality. For men, love is nothing more than gratitude for the gift of pleasure, and no one had ever given me more pleasure than Myriam. She could contract her pussy at will (sometimes softly, with a slow, irresistible pressure; sometimes in sharp, rebellious little tugs); when she gave me her little ass, she swiveled it around with infinite grace. As for her blow jobs, I'd never encountered anything like them. She approached each one as if it were her first, and would be her last. Any single one of them would have been enough to justify a man's existence.

I ended up calling her, once I'd spent a few more days wondering whether I should. We agreed to meet that very evening.

We continue to use *tu* with our ex-girlfriends, that's the custom, but we kiss them on the cheeks and not the lips. Myriam wore a short black skirt and black tights. I'd invited her to my place. I didn't really want to go to a restaurant. She had an inquisitive look around the room and sat back on the sofa. Her skirt really was extremely short and she'd put on makeup. I offered her a drink. Bourbon, she said, if you have it.

"Something's different . . ." She took a sip. "But I can't tell what."

"The curtains." I had installed double drapes, orange and ocher with a vaguely ethnic motif. I'd also bought a throw for the couch.

She turned around, kneeling on the sofa to examine the curtains. "Pretty," she decided. "Very pretty, actually. But then, you always did have good taste—for such a macho man." She turned to face me. "You don't mind me calling you macho, do you?"

"I don't know, I guess I must be kind of macho. I've never really been convinced that it was a good idea for women to get the vote, study the same things as men, go into the same professions, et cetera. I mean, we're used to it now— but was it really a good idea?"

Her eyes narrowed in surprise. For a few seconds she actually seemed to be thinking it over, and suddenly I was too, for a moment. Then I realized I had no answer, to this question or any other.

"So you're for a return to patriarchy?"

"You know I'm not *for* anything, but at least patriarchy existed. I mean, as a social system it was able to perpetuate itself. There were families with children, and most of them had children. In other words, it worked, whereas now there aren't enough children, so we're finished."

"Yes, in theory you're definitely macho. But then you have such refined tastes in writers: Mallarmé, Huysmans. They don't exactly play to the macho base. Plus you have a weirdly feminine eye for household textiles. On the other hand, you dress like a loser. I could see you cultivating a macho slob thing, but you don't like ZZ Top, you've always preferred Nick Drake. In other words, you're a walking enigma."

I poured myself another bourbon before responding. Aggression often masks a desire to seduce—I'd read that in Boris Cyrulnik, and Boris Cyrulnik isn't fucking around. When it comes to psychology, no one's got anything on him. He's like a Konrad Lorenz of human beings. Plus, her thighs had parted slightly as she waited for me to answer. This was body language, and the body doesn't lie.

"There's nothing enigmatic about it, unless you psychol-

28

ogize like a women's magazine, where everyone's reduced to some kind of consumer demographic: the eco-responsible urban professional, the brand-conscious bourgeoise, the LGBT-friendly club girl, the satanic geek, the techno-Buddhist. They invent a new one every week. I don't match up with some preconceived consumer profile, that's all."

"You know . . . the one night we see each other again, don't you think we could try to be nice?" I heard the catch in her voice and was ashmed. "Are you hungry?" I asked, to smooth things over. No, she wasn't hungry, but we always ended up eating. "Would you like sushi?" She said yes, of course. Everyone always says yes to sushi. From the most discerning gourmets to the strictest calorie counters, there's a sort of universal consensus regarding this shapeless juxtaposition of raw fish and white rice. I had a delivery menu, and she was already poring over the *wasabi* and the *maki* and the *salmon rolls*—I didn't understand a word of it, and didn't care to. I chose the B3 combination and called in the order. I should have taken her out to a restaurant after all. When I hung up, I put on Nick Drake. We sat there not saying anything for a long time, until I broke the silence by asking, idiotically enough, how school was going. She gave me a reproachful look and answered that it was going well, she was planning to get a master's in publishing. Relieved, I managed to steer the conversation toward a more general topic, which happened to validate her career goals: how even though the French economy was falling apart, publishing was doing all right and had increasing profit margins. It was amazing, even, to think that the only thing left to people in their despair was reading.

"You don't seem to be doing too great yourself. But

then you always seemed that way, really," she said without animosity, almost sadly. What could I say? I couldn't exactly argue.

"Do I really seem that depressed?" I asked after another silence.

"No, not depressed. In a sense it's worse. You've always had this weird kind of honesty, like an inability to make the compromises that everyone has to make, in the end, just to go about their lives. Let's say you're right about patriarchy, that it's the only viable solution. Where does that leave me? I'm studying, I think of myself as an individual person, endowed with the same capacity for reflection and decision-making as a man. Do you really think I'm disposable?"

The right answer was probably yes, but I kept my mouth shut. Maybe I wasn't as honest as all that. The sushi still hadn't arrived. I poured myself another bourbon, my third. Nick Drake went on evoking pure maidens, princesses of old. And I still didn't want to give her a child, or help out around the house, or buy a Baby Björn. I didn't even want to fuck her, or maybe I kind of wanted to fuck her but I also kind of wanted to die, I couldn't really tell. I felt a slight wave of nausea. Where the fuck was Rapid'Sushi, anyway? I should have asked her to suck me off, right then. Then we might have stood a chance, but I let the darkness settle and thicken, second by second.

"Maybe I should go," she said after a silence of at least three minutes. Nick Drake had just ended his lamentations. We were about to hear the belchings of Nirvana. I turned it off and said, "If you like."

"I'm really, really sorry to see you like this, François,"

she said to me in the hallway. She already had her coat on. "I'd like to help, but I don't know how. You won't even give me a chance." We kissed cheeks again. I didn't see what else we could do.

•

The sushi showed up a few minutes after she left. We'd over-ordered.

II

II

After Myriam left, I kept to myself for more than a week. For the first time since I'd been made a professor, I didn't even feel up to teaching my Wednesday classes. The intellectual summits of my life had been completing my dissertation and publishing my book, and that was already more than ten years ago. Intellectual summits? Summits, period. In those days, at least, I'd felt *justified*. Since then, all I'd produced was a few short articles for the *Journal of Nineteenth-Century Studies*, plus a couple for *The Literary Review*, when some new book touched on my field of expertise. My articles were clear, incisive, and brilliant. They were generally well received, especially since I never missed a deadline. But was that enough to justify a life? And why did a life need to be justified? Animals live without feeling the least need of justification, as do the crushing majority of men. They live because they live, and then I suppose they die because they die, and for them that's all there is to it. If only as a Huysmanist, I felt obliged to do a little better.

When doctoral students are planning to write their dissertation on a certain author and ask me in what order they should approach his works, I always tell them to privilege chronology. Not because the life has any real importance, but because, taken in order, an author's books make up a sort of intellectual biography with a logic of its own. In the case of Joris-Karl Huysmans, the obvious problem was what to do with *À rebours*. Once you've written a book of such powerful originality, unrivaled even today in all of literature, how do you go on writing?

The obvious answer is: with great difficulty. Indeed, *En rade*, which follows *À rebours*, is a disappointing book. How could it not be? And yet if its faults, its air of stagnation and slow decline, never quite overcome our pleasure in reading it, this is thanks to a stroke of genius on Huysmans's part: to recount, in a book bound to be disappointing, the story of a disappointment. The coherence between subject and treatment makes an aesthetic whole. It gets pretty boring, yes, but you keep reading, because you can feel that the characters aren't the only ones stranded in their country retreat: Huysmans is stranded there, too. It would almost seem that he was trying to go back to Naturalism—the sordid Naturalism of the countryside, where the peasants turn out to be more abject and greedy even than Parisians—if not for the dream sequences, which interrupt and ultimately hobble the story, and make it so impossible to classify.

In his next book Huysmans finally finds a way out, using a tried-and-true strategy: he adopts a main character, an authorial stand-in, whose development we follow over several books. These are all things I managed to explain clearly enough in my dissertation. The trouble was what came next, because the whole point of Durtal's development (and of Huysmans's)—from the first pages of *Là-bas*, with its farewell to Naturalism, through *En route* and *La cathédrale* and ending with *L'oblat*—is his conversion to Catholicism.

Obviously, it's not easy for an atheist to talk about a series of books whose main subject is religious conversion. In the same way, it's hard to imagine someone who has never been in love, someone to whom love is completely alien, taking an interest in a novel all about that particular passion. In the absence of any real emotional identification, what an atheist slowly comes to feel when confronted with Durtal's spiritual adventures—with the series of spiritual retreats, followed by eruptions of divine grace, that make up Huysmans's last three books—is, unfortunately, boredom.

It was at this moment in my reflections (I'd just got up and was having my coffee, waiting for the sun to rise) that I had an extremely unpleasant thought: just as *À rebours* was the summit of Huysmans's life as a writer, Myriam was undoubtedly the summit of my love life. How would I ever get over her? The only realistic answer was I wouldn't.

•

While I was waiting to die, I still had the *Journal of Nineteenth-Century Studies*. Its next meeting was in less than a week. Also, election day was coming up. Many men take an interest in politics and war, but these diversions never appealed to me. I was about as political as a bath towel. No doubt it was my loss. To be fair, when I was young, the elections could not have been less interesting; the mediocrity of the "political offerings" was almost surprising. A center-left candidate would be elected, serve either one or two terms, depending how charismatic he was, then for obscure reasons he would fail to complete a third. When people got tired of that candidate, and the center-left in general, we'd witness the phenomenon of *democratic change*, and the voters would install a candidate of the center-right, also for one or two terms, depending on his personal appeal. Western nations took a strange pride in this system, though it amounted to little more than a power-sharing deal between two rival gangs, and they would even go to war to impose it on nations that failed to share their enthusiasm.

Over the years, the rise of the far right had made things a little more interesting. It gave the debates a long-lost frisson of fascism. Still, it wasn't until 2017, and the presidential runoff, that things really started to heat up. The foreign press looked on, bewildered, as a leftist president was reelected in a country that was more and more openly right-wing: the spectacle was shameful but mathematically inevitable. Over the next few weeks a strange, oppressive mood settled over France, a kind of suffocating despair, all-encompassing but shot through with glints of insurrection. People even chose to leave the country. Then, a month after the elections, Mohammed Ben Abbes announced the creation of the Muslim Brotherhood. There had already been one attempt to form an Islamic party, the French Muslim Party, but it soon fell apart over the embarrassing anti-Semitism of its leader—so extreme that it drove him into an alliance with the far right. The Muslim Brotherhood learned its lesson and was careful to take a moderate line. It soft-pedaled its support of the Palestinians and kept up good relations with the Jewish religious authorities. As with Muslim Brotherhood parties in the Arab world—and the French Communists before them—the real political action was carried out through a network of youth groups, cultural institutions, and charities. In a country gripped by ever more widespread unemployment, the strategy broadened the Brotherhood's reach far beyond strictly observant Muslims. Its rise was nothing short of meteoric. After less than five years, it was now polling just behind the Socialists: at 21 versus 23 percent. As for the traditional right, the Union for a Popular Movement (UMP) had plateaued at 14 percent. The National Front, with 32 percent, remained far and away the leading party of France.

In recent years David Pujadas had graduated from news anchor to national icon. Not only had he joined the "select club" of political journalists (Cotta, Elkabbach, Duhamel, a few others) who alone, in the history of the media, had been deemed worthy to moderate a presidential debate between the general election and the runoff, but he had outshone all his predecessors when it came to courtesy, firmness, and calm. He knew how to shrug off an insult, how to settle a fight when it started turning into a brawl, and how to give the whole proceeding a dignified, democratic veneer. The National Front and the Muslim Brotherhood agreed to have him as their moderator, and certainly no primary debate had ever been more eagerly awaited: the Muslim Brotherhood candidate had been rising in the polls since the beginning of his campaign. If he managed to take the lead from the Socialists, the runoff would be historic, and very hard to predict. The left, despite repeated and increasingly dire calls from their own dailies and weeklies, refused to back a Muslim. The right, whose numbers continued to grow, seemed ready, despite their leaders' very firm proclamations, to cross over and support a "national unity" candidate. So Ben Abbes was playing for high stakes—no doubt the highest stakes of his life.

•

The debate took place on a Wednesday, which wasn't ideal: the day before, I'd laid in an assortment of Indian dinners and three bottles of red wine. A high-pressure system had settled over Hungary and Poland, which prevented the low-pressure system over England from moving south; across continental Europe, the weather was unseasonably cold and dry. My doctoral students had been bugging the shit out of me with their lazy questions, mainly about why minor poets (Moréas, Corbière, etc.) were considered minor, and who said they couldn't be considered major (like Baudelaire-Rimbaud-Mallarmé, then Breton). Their questions were not disinterested, far from it. They were bad students with bad attitudes—one wanted to do his dissertation on Cros, the other on Corbière—but today I could see their hearts weren't really in it, they just wanted to hear me give the establishment line. I punted, and recommended Laforgue as a compromise.

As soon as the debate started, I was fucked. Or rather, my microwave was fucked. It started doing something new (spinning around and emitting an almost inaudible hum, but without heating the food), which meant I ended up having to cook my Indian dinners on the stove and missed the opening speeches. Still, as far as I could tell, the whole thing was almost excessively polite. The two candidates for the highest office in the land showered each other with tokens of mutual respect, took turns expressing their immense love of France, and agreed about more or less everything. And yet, at the same time, clashes broke out in Montfermeil between right-wing extremists and a group of young Africans of no declared political affiliation. There had been fighting all week following the desecration of a local mosque. The next day a nativist website claimed that these last riots had been extremely violent, with several fatalities, a claim immediately disputed by the Ministry of the Interior. As always, the leaders of the National Front and Muslim Brotherhood published statements vigorously condemning any criminal acts. Two years before, when the riots started, the media had had a field day, but now people discussed them less and less. They'd become old news. For years now, probably decades, *Le Monde* and all the other center-left newspapers, which is to say every newspaper, had been denouncing the "Cassandras" who predicted civil war between Muslim immigrants and the indigenous populations of Western Europe. The way it was explained to me by a colleague in the classics department, this was an odd allusion to make. In Greek mythology, Cassandra is a very beautiful young maiden ("like the golden Aphrodite," Homer writes). Apollo, having fallen in love with her, offers her the gift of prophecy in exchange for her favors. Cassandra accepts his gift, only to refuse the god's advances. Enraged, Apollo spits in her mouth, meaning that no one will ever understand or believe anything she says. She goes on to predict the rape of Helen by Paris, then the Trojan War, and she alerts her fellow Trojans to the ruse of the Greeks (the famous "Trojan Horse") that allows them to capture the city. She winds up assassinated by Clytemnestra, but not before predicting her own murder and that of Agamemnon, who refuses to believe her. In short, Cassandra offered an example of worst-case predictions that always came true. In hindsight, the journalists of the center-left seemed only to have repeated the blindness of the Trojans. History is full of such blindness: we see it among the intellectuals, politicians, and journalists of the 1930s, all of whom were convinced that Hitler would "come to see reason." It may well be impossible for people who have lived and prospered under a given social system to imagine the point of view of those who feel it offers them nothing, and who can contemplate its destruction without any particular dismay.

But in fact, the media's attitude had changed over the last few months. No one talked about violence in the banlieues or race riots anymore. That was all passed over in silence. They'd even stopped denouncing the "Cassandras." In the end the Cassandras had gone silent, too. People were sick of the subject, and the kind of people I knew had gotten sick of it before everyone else. "What has to happen will happen" seemed to be the general feeling. The next evening, when I went to the spring launch of the *Journal of Nineteenth-Century Studies*, I knew the riots in Montfermeil would be talked about less than the presidential debates, and much less than recent university hires. The party was being held in the rue Chaptal, at the Museum of the Romantics, which had been rented for the occasion.

I'd always loved Place Saint-Georges, with its charming Belle Époque facades, and I stopped for a moment in front of the bust of Gavarni before I walked up the rue Notre-Dame-de-Lorette, then the rue Chaptal. At number sixteen I found the short, tree-lined alley that led to the museum.

It was a mild evening, and the double doors to the back garden had been left open. I helped myself to a glass of champagne, and as I stepped out under the linden trees, I spotted Alice, a lecturer at the University of Lyon III who worked on Nerval. Her delicate dress, printed with bright flowers, must have been what's called a cocktail dress. The truth is I've never quite grasped the difference between a cocktail dress and an evening dress, but I knew Alice would always wear the appropriate thing and, more generally, act the appropriate way. She was easy company, and I hurried over to say hello even though she was talking to a young man with angular features and very pale skin. He wore jeans, a blue blazer, a PSG T-shirt, and bright red sneakers. The effect was strangely elegant. He introduced himself as Godefroy Lempereur.

"I'm one of your new colleagues," he said, turning in my direction. I saw he was drinking straight whiskey. "I was just hired at Paris Three."

"So I've heard. You work on Bloy, don't you?"

"François has always detested Bloy," Alice interrupted brightly. "As a Huysmanist, naturally, he's in the other camp."

Lempereur offered me a surprisingly warm smile and said quickly, "I know who you are, of course. I'm a great admirer of your work on Huysmans." Then he paused, as if choosing his words, without once dropping his gaze. His eyes were so intense that I thought he must be wearing makeup—at the very least that had to be mascara on his eyelashes—and I had the feeling that he was about to say something important. Alice watched us with the affectionate, slightly mocking look that women get when they witness a conversation between men—that oddity, not quite buggery, or duel, but something in between. Above our heads the linden branches stirred in the breeze. Just then, in the distance, I heard a soft, muffled noise like an explosion.

"It's curious," Lempereur said finally, "that we remain so close to the chosen authors of our youth. One might think, after a century or two, that such passions should have faded, that as academics we might accede to a kind of literary objectivity, et cetera. And yet, not at all. Huysmans, Zola, Barbey, Bloy—they all knew one another, were on good terms or bad, formed allegiances, quarreled among themselves. Their shared personal history is the history of French literature, and more than a century later, we keep reenacting it. We remain loyal to our old heroes. We'll always be ready to love for their sake, to quarrel, to battle it out in opposing monographs."

"Yes, but that's a good thing. At least, it proves that literature is serious."

"Nobody ever quarreled with poor Nerval," Alice interjected, but Lempereur didn't even seem to hear her. He kept staring into my eyes, as if carried away by his own eloquence.

"You were never anything but serious," he went on. "I've read all of your articles in the *Journal*. It wasn't quite that way with me. I became fascinated with Bloy when I was twenty, fascinated by his intransigence, his violence, his virtuosic gift for scorn and insult—but it was all very much of the moment. Bloy was the ultimate weapon against the twentieth century, its mediocrity, its moronic 'engagement,' its cloying humanitarianism; against Sartre, and Camus, and all their political playacting; and against all those sickening formalists, the *nouveau roman*, the pointless absurdity of it all. So, now I'm twenty-five. I still don't like Sartre, or Camus, or anything to do with the *nouveau roman*, and yet Bloy's virtuosity seems oppressive to me, and I confess that all his blather about the spiritual and the sacred leaves me cold. Nowadays I would rather reread Maupassant or Flaubert—or even Zola, at least certain pages. And also, of course, the inimitable Huysmans . . ."

For an *intellectual of the right*, I was thinking, he was seductive enough. He'd stand out in the department, in a minor way. You can let people talk for a long time, they're always interested in what they have to say, but every now and then you're supposed to contribute. I looked over at Alice, but

45

without much hope: as a true Frühromantik, she couldn't have cared less about the fin de siècle. "You're what," I asked, "Catholic? Fascist? Both?" It just popped out. I was out of practice with intellectuals of the right—I couldn't remember how to behave. All at once, in the distance, we heard a kind of sustained crackling. "What was that, do you think?" asked Alice. "It sounded like shooting," she added, hesitantly. We fell silent, and I realized that everyone in the garden had fallen silent, too. Again I noticed the rustle of wind in the leaves, and discreet footfalls on the gravel. A few guests left the hall where the party was being held and walked out quietly under the trees, waiting. Two teachers from the University of Montpellier were standing near me. They had turned on their smartphones and were holding them strangely, the screens horizontal like sorcerers' wands. "It's nothing," one of them whispered anxiously. "They're still discussing the G20." If they thought the networks were going to cover the event, any more than they'd covered Montfermeil, they were sadly mistaken. The blackout was complete.

"That's the first fighting we've had in Paris," Lempereur remarked, in a neutral tone. Just then we heard a new round of gunfire, this time quite distinct, as if nearby, and a much louder explosion. All the guests turned toward the sound. A column of smoke was rising into the sky above the buildings. It must have been coming from somewhere near Place de Clichy.

"Well, it looks as if our little soirée is breaking up," Alice said. Indeed, many of the guests were trying to use their phones, and some had begun to move toward the exit, but slowly, one step at a time, as if to show that they were in control and would under no circumstances take part in a stampede.

"We could continue our conversation at my house, if you like," Lempereur offered. "I live nearby, in the rue Cardinal Mercier."

"I have class tomorrow in Lyon, and my train's at six," Alice said. "I'd better head home."

"Are you sure?"

"Yes. It's odd, I'm not the least bit afraid."

I looked at her, wondering whether I should insist, but strangely I wasn't afraid, either. Somehow, I don't know why, I was convinced the fighting would go no farther than the boulevard de Clichy.

•

Alice's Twingo was parked at the corner of the rue Blanche. "I'm not sure this is such a great idea," I told her, after we'd said our goodbyes. "Will you at least call me when you get home?" She said she would, and drove away. "What a remarkable woman," said Lempereur. I agreed, even as it occurred to me that I knew almost nothing about her. Apart from titles and promotions, sexual indiscretions were pretty much the only things my colleagues and I ever talked about, and yet I'd never heard so much as a whisper about Alice. She was smart, stylish, pretty—how old could she be? My age, more or less, early forties, and as far as I could tell she lived alone. She was too young to give up, I thought. Then I remembered that I'd just given up the day before. "Remarkable," I echoed, and tried to put the idea out of my mind.

The shooting had stopped. As we turned at the rue Ballu, which was deserted at this hour, we stepped back into the precise era of our favorite writers, a fact I pointed out to Lempereur. Nearly all the buildings dated from the Second Empire or the start of the Third Republic and were unusually well preserved. "It's true," he answered. "Even Mallarmé's Tuesday evenings took place just over there, in the rue de Rome. Where do you live?"

"Avenue de Choisy. Vintage nineteen seventies—an era less well-known for its writers, obviously."

"That's Chinatown, isn't it?"

"Exactly. Right in the heart of Chinatown."

He seemed to ponder it. "That may turn out to have been an intelligent choice," he said. We had reached the corner of the rue de Clichy. I stopped, transfixed. A hundred yards north of us, Place de Clichy was completely enveloped in flames; we could see the burned-out husks of cars and a bus. The statue of Maréchal Moncey, black and imposing, stood out in the middle of the blaze. There was no one in sight and no sound but the repetitive wail of a siren.

"How much do you know about the career of Maréchal Moncey?"

"Not a thing."

"He served under Napoleon. He won distinction defending the Clichy barrier against the Russians in 1814 . . . You know," Lempereur continued in the same tone, "if the ethnic fighting spreads within Paris itself, the Chinese will stay out of it. Chinatown may become one of the last safe neighborhoods in the city."

"You think that could actually happen?"

He shrugged. At that moment I was amazed to see two riot police in Kevlar, machine guns slung over their shoulders, walking calmly down the rue de Clichy toward Gare Saint-Lazare. They were chatting away, and didn't give us so much as a glance.

"They . . ." I was dumbstruck. "They're acting as if nothing's going on."

"Indeed." Lempereur had stopped and was thoughtfully stroking his chin. "At this point, it's hard to say what is, or isn't, possible. Anyone who tells you otherwise is either a fool or a liar. I don't think anyone has any idea what the next few weeks will bring. Well . . . ," he said, after another pause, "my place is up this way. I hope your friend is all right."

Quiet and deserted, the rue du Cardinal Mercier led to a fountain surrounded by colonnades. On either side stood massive entryways, mounted with surveillance cameras and, behind them, courtyards planted with trees. Lempereur touched his finger to a small aluminum plaque, which must have been a biometric reader: a metal grate rolled open before us. At the end of the courtyard, behind the plane trees, I could just make out a small *hôtel particulier*, typically Second Empire, cozy and elegant. There was no way he lived here on a teacher's salary. How did he do it?

For some reason, I'd pictured my young colleague in pared-down, minimalist surroundings, with lots of white. On the contrary, the furniture matched the building exactly. The salon was full of easy chairs upholstered in silk and velvet, the tables elaborately inlaid with marquetry and mother-of-pearl. A large, imposing painting, likely an original Bouguereau, hung over an ornate mantelpiece. I sat on a narrow ottoman with bottle-green stripes and was given a glass of pear brandy.

"If you like, we can try to find out what's going on," he offered, as he handed me the glass.

"No, I know there won't be anything on the networks. Maybe on CNN, if you have a dish."

"I've been trying. There's nothing on CNN—nothing on YouTube, either. No surprise there. Sometimes they show a few snippets on RuTube, cell-phone footage mainly, but it's very hit-or-miss. It's been days since I've been able to find anything."

"But why the blackout? I don't see what the government's thinking."

"I think they're terrified the National Front is going to win the election. Any images of urban violence mean more votes for the National Front. So now the far right is stirring things up even more. Of course the guys in the banlieues retaliate, but you'll notice that every time things have gotten out of hand these last few months, it started with an anti-Muslim provocation: somebody desecrating a mosque or forcing a woman to lift her veil, that kind of thing."

"And you think the National Front is behind it all?"

"No, no. They can't do it themselves, that's not how it works. There are, shall we say, back channels."

•

He finished his brandy and poured us each another glass in silence. The Bouguereau above the fireplace showed five women in a garden, some in white tunics, others half-nude, surrounding a nude infant with curly hair. One of the nude women hid her breasts with her hands. The other couldn't— she was holding a bouquet of wildflowers. She had lovely breasts, and the artist had executed her drapery to perfection.

It was just a little more than a century old, and that seemed so long ago that at first I felt bewildered by this incomprehensible object. Slowly, gradually, you could imagine your way into the skin of a nineteenth-century bourgeois, one of the frock-coated grandees who had commissioned the painting; you could feel, as they had, erotic stirrings before these Grecian nudes; but it was a hard, laborious climb back into the past. Maupassant, Zola, even Huysmans were much more immediately accessible. I should probably have spoken of that—of the uncanny power of literature—and yet I chose to go on discussing politics. I wanted to know more, and he seemed to know more. At least, that was the impression he gave.

"I take it you've been part of the nativist movement." I hit just the right note—that of an interested, merely curious man of the world. I was benevolently neutral. I was dashing. He gave me a big unguarded grin.

"I knew they'd been talking in the department. Yes, I belonged to a nativist organization, years ago, when I was writing my dissertation. These nativists were Catholic, in many cases royalists, nostalgics, romantics at heart—drunks, mostly. Then everything changed, and we fell out of touch. If I went to a meeting now, I doubt I'd recognize anyone there."

I maintained a tactical silence. When you maintain a tactical silence and look people right in the eye, as if drinking in their words, they talk. People like to be listened to, as every researcher knows—every researcher, every writer, every spy.

"You see," he continued, "the so-called nativist bloc was

actually anything but a bloc. It was divided into various factions, none of which got along with the others. You had Catholics, followers of Bruno Mégret, royalists, neo-pagans, hard-core secularists from the far left . . . But all that changed when the 'Indigenous Europeans' came along. They started out as a direct response to the Indigènes de la République. They had a clear, unifying message: We are the indigenous peoples of Europe, the first occupants of the land. They said, We're against Muslim occupation—and we're also against American companies and against the new capitalists from India, China, et cetera, buying up our heritage. They were clever, they quoted Geronimo, Cochise, and Sitting Bull. Above all, their website was state-of-the-art. It was really well designed. The music was catchy. It brought in new members, younger members."

"You think they actually want to start a civil war?"

"Think? I know. Here, I'll show you something they put online . . ."

He got up and went into the other room. Ever since we'd sat down in his apartment, there had been no more sounds of shooting—or else we were out of earshot, in the deep calm of that dead-end street.

He came back and handed me a dozen sheets of paper, stapled together and covered in small type. Sure enough, the headline read: GET READY FOR CIVIL WAR.

"The Web is full of this kind of thing, but here's one of the better overviews, with the most reliable statistics. There are lots of numbers, because the article looks at all twenty-two EU member states, but the conclusion is the same in every case. Basically, they argue that belief in a transcendent being conveys a genetic advantage: that couples who follow one of the three religions of the Book and maintain patriarchal values have more children than atheists or agnostics. You see less education among women, less hedonism and individualism. And to a large degree, this belief in transcendence can be passed on genetically. Conversions, or cases where people grow up to reject family values, are statistically insignificant. In the vast majority of cases, people stick with whatever metaphysical system they grow up in. That's why atheist humanism—the basis of any 'pluralist society'—is doomed. Monotheism is on the rise, especially in the Muslim population—and that's even before you factor in immigration. European nativists start by admitting that, sooner or later, we'll see a civil war between the Muslims and everybody else. They conclude that, if they want to have a fighting chance, that war had better come as soon as possible—certainly before 2050, preferably much sooner . . ."

"I see what you mean . . ."

"Yes, from a political and military standpoint they're obviously right. The question is whether they've decided to go from talk to action—and if so, in which countries. Every country in Europe is more or less equally hostile to Muslims, but France is a special case because of its military. The French armed forces are still among the strongest in the world, and their strength has been maintained, in the face of budget cuts, by one government after another. That means no uprising can take hold if the government sends in the troops. Which is why there has to be a special strategy for France."

"Meaning?"

"Soldiers have short careers. Right now, we have three hundred thirty thousand troops in the French armed forces, land, sea, and air, if you include the *gendarmerie*. Annual recruitment is roughly twenty thousand. So within fifteen years or so, we'll see a complete turnover in military personnel. If young extremists—and they're almost all young—enlist en masse, it won't be long before they seize ideological control. That's always been the strategy of the political wing. But two years ago they faced a challenge from the military wing, who want immediate armed struggle. Now, I think the political wing will stay in power—the military wing won't attract anyone but juvenile delinquents and gun nuts. But in other countries, who knows? Especially in Scandinavia. Their multiculturalism is even more oppressive than ours here in France, plus you have lots of seasoned extremists, and a negligible military. Yes, if there's going to be a general uprising anytime soon in Europe, look to Norway or Denmark, though Belgium and Holland are also zones of potential instability."

At two in the morning all was calm, and I had no trouble getting a cab. I complimented Lempereur on his brandy— we had practically finished the bottle. Like everyone else, of course, I'd spent years, decades, hearing people talk about these things. The expression *"Après moi le déluge"* has been attributed alternately to Louis XV or to his mistress Madame de Pompadour. It pretty much summarized my own state of mind, but now, for the first time, I had a troubling thought: What if the deluge came before I died? Obviously, it's not as if I expected my last years to be happy. There was no reason that I should be spared from grief, illness, or suffering. But until now I had always hoped to depart this world without undue violence.

Was he being alarmist? I didn't think he was, unfortunately. The kid struck me as a deep thinker. The next day I looked on YouTube, but there was nothing about Place de Clichy. All I could find was one video, and it was scary enough, though there was nothing actually violent about it: fifteen guys in black, hooded, armed with machine guns, marching slowly in V formation through what looked like the projects in Argenteuil. This was no cell-phone video: the resolution was very high, and someone had added a slow-motion effect. Static, imposing, shot from below, the clip could only have been meant as proof that boots were on the ground, that the territory was under control. If there was an ethnic conflict, I'd automatically be lumped together with the whites, and for the first time, as I went out to buy groceries, I was grateful to the Chinese for having always kept the neighborhood free of blacks or Arabs—of pretty much anyone who wasn't Chinese, apart from a few Vietnamese.

Still, it would be prudent to come up with an evacuation plan, in case things took a sudden turn for the worse. My father lived in a chalet in the Massif des Écrins. He had just moved in with someone (at least, I'd just found out about her). My mother was living out her depression in Nevers, alone except for her bulldog. These two baby boomers had always been completely self-centered, and I had no reason to think they'd willingly take me in. Occasionally I found myself wondering whether I'd ever see my parents again before they died, but the answer was always negative, and I didn't think even a civil war could bring us together. They'd find some pretext for refusing to shelter me. They never had any shortage of pretexts. I'd had a handful of friends over the years, kind of, but we weren't really in touch. There was Alice. I supposed I could call Alice a friend. All in all, now that Myriam and I had broken up, I was very much alone.

Sunday, May 15

I've always loved election night. I'd go so far as to say it's my favorite TV show, after the World Cup finals. Obviously there was less suspense in elections, since, according to their peculiar narrative structure, you knew from the first minutes how they would end, but the wide range of actors (the political scientists, the pundits, the crowds of supporters cheering or in tears at party headquarters . . . and the politicians, in the heat of the moment, with their thoughtful or passionate declarations) and the general excitement of the participants really gave you the feeling, so rare, so precious, so telegenic, that history was coming to you live.

To avoid a repeat of the last debate, which I'd spent dealing with my microwave, I bought taramasalata, hummus, blini, and salmon roe. The day before, I'd stocked the refrigerator with two bottles of Rully. As soon as David Pujadas went on the air at 7:50, I knew this election night would be top-notch, and that I was about to experience some exceptional TV. Pujadas was always very professional, of course, but there was no mistaking the gleam in his eye: the results, which he already knew, and which in ten minutes he'd be allowed to divulge, had come as a shock. The French political landscape was about to be turned upside down.

"Tonight will go down in history," he began, as they reported the first returns. The National Front was way ahead, with 34.1 percent of the vote. That part was more or less expected. It was what the polls had said all month—Marine Le Pen had gained only a few points in the last weeks of the campaign. But behind her, the Socialists had 21.8 percent and the Muslim Brotherhood 21.7 percent—they were neck and neck. With such a slim margin, they could easily switch positions, and probably would several times before the night was over: so far only the polling stations in Paris and the other big cities had reported. With 12.1 percent of the vote, the conservative Union for a Popular Movement was clearly out of the running.

•

Their candidate, Jean-François Copé, didn't appear onscreen until 9:50. Haggard, badly shaven, tie askew, he looked even more than usual as if he'd just been through an interrogation. With pained humility, he agreed that the conservatives had suffered a setback, a serious setback, and that he took full responsibility, though he didn't go so far as to say he was retiring from politics, like Lionel Jospin in 2002. As for which candidate the UMP would support in the runoff, he said only that the executive bureau of the party would meet in a week to make their determination.

At ten o'clock neither the Socialists nor the Muslim

Brotherhood had pulled ahead. The latest results showed them in a dead heat. This state of uncertainty spared the Socialist candidate from having to give what would have been a difficult speech. Was it really all over for the two parties that had dominated French political life since the birth of the Fifth Republic? The prospect was so amazing that, as the commentators blew by, you could see they all secretly wanted it to happen—even David Pujadas, whom no one suspected of being especially friendly to Islam, and who was said to be friends with Manuel Valls. Christophe Barbier, flashing around his trademark red scarf, was without question the star pundit of the night: he appeared on one channel after another so fast that he seemed to enjoy the gift of ubiquity, and kept the scarf trick going until a very late hour, easily eclipsing the ashen Renaud Dély, whose *Observateur* had failed to predict the upset, and even Yves Thréard, of *Le Figaro*, who usually put up a better fight.

It was just after midnight, as I finished my second bottle of Rully, that they announced the final results: Mohammed Ben Abbes, the candidate of the Muslim Brotherhood, had come in second with 22.3 percent of the vote. With 21.9 percent, the Socialists were out. Manuel Valls gave a short, very sober speech congratulating the two winners. Pending a meeting of the Socialist leadership, he withheld any endorsement.

When I went in to teach class, I finally felt that something might happen, that the political system I'd grown up with, which had been showing cracks for so long, might suddenly explode. I don't know exactly where the feeling came from. Maybe it was the attitude of my grad students: even the most apathetic and apolitical looked tense, anxious. They were obviously searching their smartphones and tablets for any news they could find. At least, they were even more checked out than usual. It may also have been the way the girls in burkas carried themselves. They moved slowly and with new confidence, walking down the very middle of the hallway, three by three, as if they were already in charge.

I was equally struck by my colleagues' lack of concern. They seemed completely unworried, as if none of this had anything to do with them. It only confirmed what I'd always thought—that, for all their education, university professors can't even imagine political developments having any effect on their careers: they consider themselves untouchable.

At the end of the day, as I turned down rue de Santeuil on my way to the metro, I caught sight of Marie-Françoise. I almost ran to catch up with her, and after a quick hello I asked her straight out: "Do you think our colleagues are right to be so calm? Are our jobs really that safe?"

"Ah!" she exclaimed, with a gnomelike grimace that did nothing to improve her looks, and lit a Gitane. "I was starting to think everyone in the whole fucking place was asleep. Our jobs are certainly *not* safe, not by a long shot, and I know whereof I speak . . ."

She considered for a moment, then replied. "My husband works at the DGSI." I gazed at her in wonder. It was the first time, in all the ten years I'd known her, that I realized she had once been a woman—that she still was a woman, in a sense—and that once upon a time a man had felt desire for this squat, stumpy, almost froglike little thing. Fortunately, she misread my look. "I know," she said, with satisfaction. "Everyone's always surprised . . . You do know what the DGSI is, don't you?"

"Intelligence, right? Kind of like the DST?"

"There is no DST anymore. It merged with police intelligence to form the DCRI, which then became the DGSI."

"Your husband's a kind of spy?"

"Not really, the spies are mainly at the DGSE, in the Ministry of Defense. The DGSI is part of the Ministry of the Interior."

"So they're like secret police?"

She smiled again, this time more discreetly, which was an improvement. "They don't call themselves that, officially—but basically, yes. One of their main jobs is to keep an eye on extremist movements, the ones that could turn terrorist. You should come by the house for a drink, my husband can tell you all about it. At least, he'll tell you as much as is allowed. I can never keep track of what's classified. In any case, big changes are in store after the elections, and believe me, they'll feel them at school."

•

They lived in Square Vermenouze, a five-minute walk from the university. Her husband didn't look anything like my idea of a secret agent (but what had I imagined, after all? some kind of Corsican, I guess, part gangster, part Ricard salesman). He was a neat, smiling man, with a skull so smooth it looked polished. He wore a plaid smoking jacket, but I could see him in a bow tie at the office, possibly a vest. Everything about him exuded an old-fashioned elegance. From the moment I saw him, I got an impression of nearly abnormal brain power. He was probably the only graduate of the École Normale ever to have passed the entrance exam for the police academy. "As soon as I received my commission, I asked to be assigned to police intelligence. It was a calling, you might say," he added with a little smile, as if secret operations were a sort of consuming hobby.

He bided his time, taking a first sip of port, then a second, before he continued:

"The negotiations between the Socialists and the Muslim Brotherhood are much trickier than expected. The Muslims are ready to cede more than half the ministries—even key ministries, like finance and the interior. That's not the trouble. On the economy and fiscal policy, they and the Socialists see eye to eye. The same goes for security, and what's more the Muslims can actually bring order to the banlieues. In foreign policy, they want France to take a slightly firmer stance against Israel, but that's hardly a problem for the left. The real difficulty, the sticking point, is education. Support for education is an old Socialist tradition, and teachers are the one profession that has stood by the party, right to the end; but now the Socialists are dealing with people who care about education even more than they do, and who won't back down. The Muslim Brotherhood is an unusual party, you know. Many of the usual political issues simply don't matter to them. To start with, the economy is not their main concern. What they care about is birthrate and education. To them it's simple—whichever segment of the population has the highest birthrate, and does the best job of transmitting its values, wins. If you control the children, you control the future. So the one area in which they absolutely insist on having their way is the education of children."

"But what do they want?"

"They want every French child to have the option of a Muslim education, at every level of schooling. Now, however you look at it, a Muslim education is very different from a secular one. First off, no coeducation. And women would only be allowed to study certain things. What the Muslim Brotherhood really wants is for most women to study home ec, once they finish grade school, then get married as soon as possible—with a small minority studying art or literature first. That's their vision of an ideal society. Also, every teacher would have to be Muslim. No exceptions. Schools would observe Muslim dietary laws and the five daily prayers; above all, the curriculum itself would have to reflect the teachings of the Koran."

"You think the Socialists will give in?"

"They haven't got much choice. If they don't reach an agreement, they don't stand a chance against the National Front. Even if they do reach an agreement, the National Front could still win. You've seen the polls. Suppose Copé refuses to vote for either party, even so, eighty-five percent of the center-right will vote National Front. It's going to be close, extremely close—fifty-fifty, really.

"So their only chance is to adopt a two-track education system. They'll probably model it on the polygamy agreement, which will maintain civil marriage as a union between two people, men or women, but will also recognize Muslim marriage—and ultimately polygamy—even though it isn't administered by the state, and will come with the same benefits and tax exemptions."

"Are you sure? That sounds so drastic . . ."

"Quite sure. It's all been settled. And it is exactly in line with the theory of minority sharia, which the Muslim Brotherhood has always embraced. So they could do something similar with education. Public education would still be available to everyone—though with vastly reduced funding. The national budget would be slashed by two-thirds at least, and this time the teachers wouldn't be able to stop it. In the current economic climate, any budget cut is bound to play well at the polls. At the same time we'd have a parallel system of Muslim charter schools. They'd have all the same accreditations as the public schools—with the difference that they could receive private funding. Obviously, the public schools would soon become second-class. Parents who cared at all about their children's future would sign them up for a Muslim education."

"The same goes for the universities," said his wife. "The Sorbonne would be a huge coup—Saudi Arabia is ready with an almost unlimited endowment. We're going to be one of the richest universities in the world."

"And Rediger will be named president?" I asked her, remembering our previous conversation.

"Oh yes. It's even more certain than before. For the last twenty years he has been unwaveringly pro-Muslim."

"He even converted, if memory serves," said her husband.

I drained my glass and he refilled it. That really would be a change.

"I imagine all of this must be top secret . . . ," I said, after I'd taken a moment to think it over. "I don't quite see why you're telling me."

"Ordinarily, I'd keep it to myself. But it's already been leaked. That's what worries us. I could read everything I just told you, and more, on certain blogs maintained by the far right. We've been infiltrated." He shook his head, as if incredulous. "They couldn't have found out more if they'd bugged the most secure offices of the Ministry of the Interior. The information is explosive, but they haven't done anything with it. That's the worst part. They haven't gone to the press. They haven't made any public announcements. They're just sitting on it. The situation is unprecedented— and really quite alarming."

I wanted to hear a little bit more about the nativist movement, but it was clear that he'd said all he was going to say.

I had a colleague, I told him, who had belonged to a nativist organization, then broke with them completely. "Yes, that's what they all say," he sneered. When I tried to ask whether some of these groups were armed, he sipped his port, then grumbled, "We've heard talk of funding from Russian oligarchs—but nothing's been confirmed." The subject was closed. I left a few minutes later.

The next day I went by the university, even though I had nothing to do there, and I called Lempereur's office. According to my calculations, he would have just gotten out of class. He picked up, and I asked him if he wanted to get a drink. He didn't care for the cafés near the university, and he suggested we meet at Delmas, in Place de la Contrescarpe.

As I walked up the rue Mouffetard, I thought more about what I'd heard from Marie-Françoise's husband. Was it possible my young colleague knew more than he'd told me? Was he still involved in the movement?

With its leather club chairs, dark floors, and red curtains, Delmas was exactly his kind of place. He would never have set foot in the café across the street, the Contrescarpe, with its annoying fake bookshelves. He was a man of taste. He ordered a glass of champagne, I ordered a Leffe, and suddenly, something in me gave way. I was sick of my own subtlety and moderation. I got straight to the point, without even waiting till we had our drinks: "The political situation seems very unstable. Tell me honestly, what would you do in my shoes?"

Although he smiled at my candor, he answered just as bluntly: "First off, I'd open a new bank account."

"A bank account—why?" It came out almost as a yelp, I must have been even more on edge than I'd realized. The waiter came back with our drinks. Lempereur paused before he answered, "It's not clear that the recent actions of the Socialist Party will go down well with their supporters . . . ," and all of a sudden I realized that he *knew*, that he was still deep in the movement, maybe even one of its leaders: he knew all about the secret leaks. For all I knew, he was the one who decided to keep them secret.

"Under the circumstances," he went on softly, "the National Front may well win the runoff. If they do, their supporters will force them to pull France out of the EU, and abandon the euro. It may turn out to be a very good thing for the economy, but in the short term we'll see some serious convulsions in the markets. It's not clear that French banks, even the biggest ones, could hang on. So I'd suggest you open an account with a foreign bank—ideally an English one, like Barclays or HSBC."

"That's it?"

"That's not nothing. Do you have a place in the country where you can go to ground?"

"No, not really."

"Even so, I'd urge you to take off, sooner rather than later. Find a little hotel somewhere. Didn't you say you lived in Chinatown? I doubt we'll see any looting or rioting near you, but all the same, I'd take a vacation and wait for things to settle down."

"I'd feel kind of like a rat abandoning ship."

"Rats are intelligent mammals," he answered calmly,

almost with amusement. "They will probably outlive us. Their society, at any rate, is a good deal more stable than ours."

"The school year isn't over. I still have two weeks of class."

"The school year!" Now he was grinning, almost laughing. "It's true that all sorts of things could happen, and nobody knows just what, but I do doubt we'll make it to the end of the school year!"

•

Now he fell silent and sipped his champagne, and I knew I'd get nothing more out of him. A slightly contemptuous smile played over his lips, which was odd, since I'd have said he was almost starting to be nice to me. I ordered another beer, this time raspberry flavored. I had no desire to go home. There was nothing and no one waiting for me there. I wondered whether Lempereur had a partner, or at least a girlfriend. Probably. He was a kind of éminence grise, a political leader, in a clandestine movement. Everyone knows there are girls who go for that kind of thing. There are girls who go for Huysmanists, for that matter. I once met a girl—a pretty, attractive girl—who told me she fantasized about Jean-François Copé. It took me several days to get over it. Really, with girls today, all bets are off.

70

Friday, May 20

The next day I opened an account at the Barclays bank in the avenue des Gobelins. The funds would be transferred in just one working day, the bank officer informed me. A few minutes later I had a Visa, very much to my surprise.

I decided to walk home. I had filled out the paperwork mechanically, on autopilot, and now I needed to think. Crossing Place d'Italie, I was overcome by the feeling that everything could disappear. That petite black woman with the curly hair and the tight jeans, waiting for the 21 bus, could disappear; she *would* disappear, or at least she'd be in for some serious reeducation. There were the usual fund-raisers in front of the Italie 2 shopping center—today they were Greenpeace—and they would disappear, too. I blinked as a bearded young man with long brown hair came up to me holding his clipboard, and it was as if he were already gone. I passed by without seeing him and went through the glass doors that led to the ground floor of the mall.

Inside, the results were more mixed. The Bricorama would

stay, but the Jennyfer's days were numbered. It had nothing to offer the good Muslim tween. Secret Stories, which advertised name-brand lingerie at discount prices, had nothing to worry about: the same kind of shops were doing fine in the malls of Riyadh and Abu Dhabi. Neither, for that matter, did Chantal Thomass or La Perla. Hidden all day in impenetrable black burkas, rich Saudi women transformed themselves by night into birds of paradise with their corsets, their see-through bras, their G-strings with multicolored lace and rhinestones. They were exactly the opposite of Western women, who spent their days dressed up and looking sexy to maintain their social status, then collapsed in exhaustion once they got home, abandoning all hope of seduction in favor of clothes that were loose and shapeless. All of a sudden, as I stood in front of the Rapid'Jus (whose concoctions kept getting more and more complicated: they had coconut-passionfruit-guava, mango-lychee-guarana, and a dozen other flavors, all with bewildering vitamin ingredients), I thought of Bruno Deslandes. I hadn't seen him in twenty years. I hadn't thought of him, either. We'd been doctoral students together, we'd even been what you might call friendly. He worked on Laforgue. His dissertation had received a pass without distinction, and soon afterward he'd gotten a job as a tax inspector, then married a girl named Annelise, whom he'd probably met at some student function. She worked in the marketing department of a mobile network, she made much more than he did, but he had job security, as they say. They'd bought a house in a subdivision in Montigny-le-Bretonneux, and they already had two kids, a boy and a girl. He was the only one in our program who'd wound up with a normal family life. The others drifted around, with a little online dating here, a little speed dating there, and a lot of solitude in between. I'd bumped into Bruno on the commuter train, and he'd invited me over the following Friday for a barbecue. It was late June, he had a backyard, he could have people over for barbecues. There would be a few neighbors but, he cautioned me, "nobody from school."

Their mistake, I realized as soon as I set foot in his backyard and said hello to his wife, was choosing a Friday night. She'd been working all day and was exhausted, plus she'd been watching too many reruns of *Come Dine with Me* on channel M6 and had planned a menu that was much too ambitious. The morel soufflé was a lost cause, but just when it became clear that even the guacamole was ruined and I thought she was going to break down in sobs, her three-year-old son started screaming at Bruno, who'd gotten shit-faced as soon as the first guests arrived and couldn't manage to turn the sausages on the grill, so I helped him out. From the depths of her despair she gave me a look of profound gratitude. It was more complicated than I'd thought, barbecuing: before I knew it, the lamb chops were covered in a film of charred fat, blackish and probably carcinogenic, the flames were leaping higher and higher but I didn't have any idea what to do, if I fiddled with the thing the bottle of butane could explode, we were alone before the mound of charred meat, and the other guests were emptying the bottles of rosé, oblivious. I was relieved to see the storm clouds gathering overhead. When we felt the first drops, wind-driven and icy, we beat a hasty retreat to the living room, where the barbecue turned into a cold buffet. As she sank down into her sofa, glaring at the tabbouleh, I thought about Annelise's life—and the life of every Western woman. In the morning she probably blow-dried her hair, then she thought about what to wear, as befitted her professional status, whether "stylish" or "sexy," most likely "stylish" in her case. Either way, it was a complex calculation, and it must have taken her a while to get ready before dropping the kids off at day care, then she spent the day e-mailing, on the phone, in various meetings, and once she got home, around nine, exhausted (Bruno was the one who picked the kids up, who made them dinner—he had the hours of a civil servant), she'd collapse, get into a sweatshirt and yoga pants, and that's how she'd greet her lord and master, and some part of him must have known—had to have known—that he was fucked, and some part of her must have known that she was fucked, and that things wouldn't get better over the years. The children would get bigger, the demands at work would increase, as if automatically, not to mention the sagging of the flesh.

I was one of the last to leave. I even helped Annelise with the cleanup. I had no intention of trying anything with her— which would have been possible. In her situation, anything was possible. I just wanted her to feel a sense of solidarity: solidarity in vain.

•

Bruno and Annelise must be divorced by now. That's how it goes nowadays. A century ago, in Huysmans's time, they would have stayed together, and maybe they wouldn't have been so unhappy after all. When I got home I poured myself a big glass of wine and plunged back into *En ménage*. I remembered it as one of Huysmans's best books, and from the first page, even after twenty years, I found my pleasure in reading it was miraculously intact. Never, perhaps, had the tepid happiness of an old couple been so lovingly described: "André and Jeanne soon felt nothing but blessed tenderness, maternal satisfaction, at sharing the same bed, at simply lying close together and talking before they turned back to back and went to sleep." It was beautiful, but was it realistic? Was it a viable prospect today? Clearly, it was connected with the pleasures of the table: "Gourmandise entered their lives as a new interest, brought on by their growing indifference to the flesh, like the passion of priests who, deprived of carnal joys, quiver before delicate viands and old wines." Certainly, in an era when a wife bought and peeled the vegetables herself, trimmed the meat, and spent hours simmering the stew, a tender and nurturing relationship could take root; the evolution of comestible conditions had caused us to forget this feeling, which, in any case, as Huysmans frankly admits, is a weak substitute for the pleasures of the flesh. In his own life, he never set up house with one of these "good little cooks" whom Baudelaire considered, along with whores, the only kind of wife a writer should have—an especially sensible observation when you consider that a whore can always turn herself into a good little cook over time, that this is even her secret desire, her natural bent. Instead, after a period of "debauchery" (these things being relative), Huysmans turned to the monastic life, and that's where he and I parted ways. I picked up *En route*, tried to read a few pages, then went back to *En ménage*. I was almost completely lacking in spiritual fiber, which was a shame since the monastic life still existed, unchanged over the centuries. As for the good little cooks, where were they now? In Huysmans's day they still existed, certainly, but because he moved in literary circles he never met them. The university wasn't much better, to tell the truth. Take Myriam, for example. Could she turn herself into a good little cook over the years? I was pondering the question when my cell phone rang, and oddly enough it was her. I stammered in surprise, I'd never actually expected her to call. I looked over at the alarm clock, it was already six p.m. I'd been so absorbed in my reading, I'd forgotten to eat. On the other hand, I also noticed that I'd practically finished my second bottle of wine.

"I thought we . . ." She hesitated. "I thought we might get together tomorrow."

"Really . . . ?"

"Tomorrow's your birthday. Did you forget?"

"Yes. Yes, to tell the truth, I'd forgotten all about it."

"And also . . ." She hesitated again. "There's something I have to tell you. And it would be good to see you, too."

Saturday, May 21

I woke at four in the morning. After Myriam had called, I'd finished _En ménage_, the book was indisputably a masterpiece, I'd hardly gotten three hours of sleep. The woman Huysmans looked for all his life he had already described when he was twenty-seven or -eight, in _Marthe_, his first novel, published in Brussels in 1876. He wanted a good little cook who could also turn herself into a whore, and he wanted this on a fixed schedule. It didn't seem so hard, turning into a whore, it seemed easier than making a good béarnaise, yet he sought this woman in vain. For the moment, I wasn't doing much better. It's not that I minded turning forty-four, it was just another birthday, except that Huysmans was forty-four years old, exactly, when he found God. From July 12 through July 20, 1892, he paid his first visit to Igny Abbey, in the Marne. On July 14 he made confession, after much hesitation, which hesitation he scrupulously recounts in _En route_. On July 15, for the first time since he was a boy, he took communion.

While I was writing my dissertation on Huysmans, I'd spent a week at Ligugé Abbey, where he eventually took lay orders, and another week at Igny Abbey. Although Igny was completely destroyed during the First World War, my stay there had been a great help to me. The decor and the furniture, modernized of course, had retained the same simplicity, the nakedness that impressed Huysmans, and the daily schedule of the various prayers and offices was unchanged, from the Angelus at four in the morning to the Salve Regina at night. Meals were taken in silence, which was very restful after the university cafeteria; and I remembered that the monks made chocolate and macaroons. Their handiwork, recommended by the Petit Futé, could be found all over France.

I could easily understand how someone might be attracted to the monastic life, even though I didn't see things the way Huysmans did, at all. I couldn't share the disgust he claimed to feel for the carnal passions. I couldn't even make sense of it. Generally speaking, my body was the seat of various painful afflictions—headaches, rashes, toothaches, hemorrhoids—that followed one after another, without interruption, and almost never left me in peace—and I was only forty-four! What would it be like when I was fifty, sixty, older? I'd be no more than a jumble of organs in slow decomposition, my life an unending torment, grim, joyless, and mean. When you got right down to it, my dick was the one organ that hadn't presented itself to my consciousness through pain, only through pleasure. Modest but robust, it had always served me faithfully. Or, you could argue, I had served it—if so, its yoke had been easy. It never gave me orders. It sometimes encouraged me to get out more, but it encouraged me humbly, without bitterness or anger. This past evening, I knew, it had interceded on Myriam's behalf. It had always enjoyed good relations with Myriam, Myriam had always treated it with affection and respect, and this had given me an enormous amount of pleasure. And sources of pleasure were hard to come by. In the end, my dick was all I had. My interest in the life of the mind had greatly diminished; my social life was hardly more satisfying than the life of my body; it, too, presented itself as a series of petty annoyances—clogged sink, slow Wi-Fi, points on my license, dishonest cleaning woman, mistakes in my tax return—and these, too, followed one after another without interruption, and almost never left me in peace. In the monastery, I imagined, one left most of these worries behind. One laid down the burden of one's individual existence. One renounced pleasure, too, but there was a case to be made for that. It was a shame, I thought while I read, that Huysmans spent so much of *En route* insisting on his disgust at the debauches in his past. Here, perhaps, he hadn't been completely honest. What attracted him about the monastery, I suspected, wasn't so much that one escaped from the quest after carnal pleasures; it was more that one could be freed from the exhausting and dreary succession of aggravations that made up daily life, from everything that he had described with such mastery in *À vau-l'eau*. In the monastery, at least, one was assured of room and board—and, best-case scenario, eternal life as a bonus.

•

Myriam came over at seven. "Happy birthday, François . . . ," she said in a tiny little voice when I opened the door, then she threw herself into my arms. Our lips and tongues met in a long, voluptuous kiss. As I walked her into the living room, I saw she was dressed even more sexily than last time. She had on another black miniskirt, even shorter than the one before, and stockings: when she sat down on the sofa I could see a garter, black against the top of her very white thigh. Her blouse, also black, was very sheer. I could see her breasts moving underneath. I realized that my fingers could still recall the touch of her aureoles. She offered a hesitant smile. There was something momentous and undecided in the air.

"Did you bring me a present?" I asked, in what I hoped was a joking tone of voice, to lighten things up.

"No," she answered gravely. "I couldn't find anything that seemed right."

After another silence, she suddenly spread her thighs wide; she was naked under her skirt, and it was so short that I could see the line of her pussy, waxed and nakedly innocent. "I'm giving you a blow job," she said, "a good one. Come here, sit on the edge of the sofa."

I obeyed, letting her undress me. She kneeled down and began by tonguing my asshole, slowly and tenderly, then she took me by the hand and raised me to my feet. I leaned back against the wall. She kneeled down again and began licking my balls, all the while jacking me off with short quick strokes.

"Tell me when you want me to suck you," she said, pausing. I waited and waited, until my desire overwhelmed me. "Now," I said.

I looked her in the eye just before she touched her tongue

to my cock; seeing her do it turned me on even more. She was in a strange state, a frenzy of concentration, as her tongue swirled over my glans, now fast, now hard and slow; she squeezed the base of my dick in her left hand, and with her right hand she stroked my balls. Waves of pleasure surged and swept over me. I could hardly stand, I was about to faint. Just before I exploded into a cry, I found the strength to beg her, "Stop . . . Stop . . ." I hardly recognized my own voice—it was distorted, almost inaudible.

"You don't want to come in my mouth?"

"No—not now."

"All right . . . I hope that means you'll want to fuck me later on. Let's have something to eat."

This time I'd ordered the sushi in advance. It had been sitting in the refrigerator since mid-afternoon. I'd also chilled two bottles of champagne.

"You know, François . . . ," she said, after she'd taken a first sip, "I'm not a whore. I'm not a nymphomaniac, either. When I go down on you, it's because I love you. I do love you, do you know that?"

I did. And I knew there was something else, something she hadn't yet told me. I looked deep into her eyes, but I didn't find a way to ask what was the matter. She finished her champagne, sighed, poured another, and said: "My parents are leaving the country."

I was speechless. She drained her glass and poured herself a third.

"They're emigrating to Israel. They fly to Tel Aviv on Friday. They're not even waiting for the runoffs. The crazy part is, they've done it all behind our backs, completely in secret. They opened a bank account in Israel, they lined up an apartment, my father cashed out his pension, they put the house up for sale, and they never said a word to any of us. My little sister and brother I could maybe understand, they're pretty young, but I'm twenty-two years old and they didn't even consult me. They're not forcing me to go with them. If I insist, they'll rent me a room in Paris, but we do have the summer break coming up, and I don't see how I can leave them, not right now. They're too scared. I hadn't really noticed till now, but in the last few months they've stopped going out. The only people they still see are other Jews. They stay in at night, working each other up—and they're not the only ones, they've got at least five other friends who've sold everything so they can move to Israel. We spent a whole night arguing about it, but they've made up their minds. They're convinced that something really bad is going to happen to Jews in France. It's weird, it's like a delayed reaction fifty years after the war. I told them they're being idiots, the National Front stopped being anti-Semitic a long time ago . . ."

"It wasn't all that long ago. You're too young to remember, but the father, Jean-Marie Le Pen, he still had connections to the old French far right. He was a drunk and a total philistine, it's not as if he'd read Drumont or Maurras, but I'm sure he heard people talk about them. They were part of his mental landscape. The daughter doesn't even know who they are, obviously. At any rate, even if the Muslim wins, I don't think you've got much to worry about. He's still allied with the Socialists, he can't just do whatever he wants . . ."

"Hmm . . ." She shook her head, unconvinced. "I guess

I'm less optimistic than you are. When a Muslim party comes to power, it's never good for the Jews. Can you think of a time it was?"

I let this go. I didn't really know much about history. I hadn't paid attention in high school, and since then I'd never managed to read a history book, at any rate, not all the way through.

She poured another glass. That was certainly the thing to do, considering—to get slightly drunk. Besides, it was good champagne.

"My brother and sister can attend the French school, and I could go to Tel Aviv University. They'd take my credits. But what am I going to do in Israel? I don't speak a word of Hebrew. France is my home."

Her voice changed, I could tell she was on the edge of tears. "I love France," she said, in a more and more broken voice, "I love . . . I don't know . . . I love the cheese."

"I have some!" I bounded to my feet clownishly, trying to defuse the situation, and went to look in the refrigerator. In point of fact, I had picked up some Saint-Marcellin, some Comté, some Bleu des Causses. I also opened a bottle of white wine, but she didn't even notice.

"And also . . . and also, I don't want us to break up," she said, then she started to sob. I went to her and held her in my arms. I couldn't think what to say. I led her to the bedroom and held her again. She went on softly crying.

•

I woke around four. There was a full moon out, and it shone brightly in the bedroom. Myriam lay on her stomach, in a

T-shirt. The boulevard was practically empty. After two or three minutes a Renault Trafic minivan rolled up in front of the apartment tower. Two Chinese men got out to smoke a cigarette, looked around, then for no apparent reason climbed back into the minivan and drove off toward Porte d'Italie. I went back to bed and caressed her ass. She pressed herself against me but didn't wake up.

I turned her over, spread her thighs, and touched her pussy; almost immediately, she was wet, and I slipped inside her. She had always liked this simple position. I lifted her legs so I could go deep, and I started to move in and out. People often describe a woman's pleasure as complex, mysterious; but for me, the workings of my own pleasure were even more unknown. All at once I felt that I could control myself as long as I had to, that I could deliberately hold back the pleasure mounting inside me. My thrusts were smooth, relentless, and after a few minutes she began to moan, then to scream. I kept moving inside her, even after her pussy started to contract around my cock. I took slow, easy breaths—I felt eternal—then she gave a very long groan and I threw myself on her and clasped her in my arms, while she said, "My love . . . my love . . . ," over and over through her tears.

I woke up again around eight, started the coffee machine, and went back to bed. Myriam's regular breathing added a slow accompaniment to the discreet gurgle of percolation. Chubby little cumulus clouds drifted across the sky. For me these had always been the clouds of happiness, the kind whose brilliant whiteness only heightens the blue of the sky, the kind children draw when they represent an ideal cottage, with a smoking chimney, a lawn, and flowers. I don't know quite why I turned on iTélé once I'd poured my first cup of coffee. The sound was up too loud, and it took me a second to find the remote so I could mute it. But it was too late, she'd already woken up. She came out into the living room, still in her T-shirt, and curled up on the sofa. Our brief moment of peace was over. I unmuted the sound. Overnight, the news had spread online about the secret negotiations between the Socialists and the Muslim Brotherhood. On every channel, from iTélé to BFM to LCI, it was all anyone was talking about. Manuel Valls had yet to comment, but Ben Abbes was going to hold a press conference at eleven.

When you saw this round, twinkling-eyed man, so mischievous with members of the press, it was easy to forget
that he'd been one of youngest students ever admitted to
the École Polytechnique, or that he'd been a classmate of
Laurent Wauquiez at the École Nationale d'Administration
in 2001, the year the students honored Nelson Mandela as
their class patron. Ben Abbes had the kindly look of a neighborhood grocer—which is just what his father had been, a
Tunisian neighborhood grocer, although his shop was on
a tony street in Neuilly-sur-Seine, not the Eighteenth Arrondissement, much less the ghettos of Bezons or Argenteuil.

No one, Ben Abbes reminded us, had benefited from our
republican meritocracy more than he had. He had no wish
to undermine a system to which he owed everything, even
the supreme honor of asking the French people for their
vote. He recalled doing his homework in the little apartment over the family shop. He briefly invoked the memory
of his father, with just the right touch of emotion. I thought
he was superb.

But, he went on, everyone had to admit that times had
changed. More and more families—whether Jewish, Christian, or Muslim—wanted their children's education to go
beyond the mere transmission of knowledge, to include spiritual instruction in their own traditions. This return to religion was deep, it crossed sectarian lines, and public education
could no longer afford to ignore it. It was time to broaden
the idea of republican schooling, to bring it into harmony
with the great spiritual traditions—Muslim, Christian, or
Jewish—of our country.

He spoke for ten minutes, in a smooth and purring voice,

then he took questions. I'd often noticed how even the most tenacious, aggressive reporters went soft in the presence of Ben Abbes, as if hypnotized. And yet it seemed to me there were some tough questions to be asked—about the ban on coeducation, for example, or the fact that teachers would have to convert to Islam. But wasn't that how it already was with Catholics? Did you have to be baptized to teach in a Christian school? On reflection, I realized I didn't know the first thing about it. By the end of the press conference, I felt that I was right where the Muslim candidate wanted me, in a state of free-floating doubt. Not only did none of this sound scary, none of it sounded especially new.

•

Marine Le Pen counterattacked at twelve thirty. Brisk and blow-dried, shot from below, with the Hôtel de Ville rising up behind her, she was almost beautiful. This was quite a contrast to her earlier appearances. During the 2017 campaign, the National Front candidate had been persuaded that a woman had to look like Angela Merkel to win the presidency, and she did all she could to match the bristling respectability of the German chancellor, right down to copying the cut of her suits. But on this May afternoon, Le Pen seemed to have recovered a flamboyance, a revolutionary élan, that recalled the origins of the movement. For a while there'd been rumors that Renaud Camus was writing some of her speeches, under the direction of Florian Phillipot. I don't know whether there was anything to that; in any case, her public speaking had certainly improved. Right away I was struck by the republican, even anticlerical, tenor of her remarks. Skipping the usual reference to Jules Ferry and the secularist reforms of the 1880s, she went all the way back to Condorcet and the historic speech he made before the Legislative Assembly in 1792, when he evoked the ancient Egyptians and Indians "among whom the human spirit made such progress, and who fell back into the most brutal and shameful ignorance the moment that religious power assumed the right to educate men."

"I thought she was a Catholic," Myriam said.

"She may be, but not her voters. The National Front never caught on with the Catholics—they care too much about welfare and the Third World. So she's adapting."

She looked at her watch and stretched, wearily. "I have to go, François. I told my parents I'd be back in time for lunch."

"They know you're here?"

"Oh, yeah. They won't be worried—it's just that they won't eat until I get there."

I'd visited her parents once, when we were first going out. They lived in a house in the Cité des Fleurs, behind the Brochant metro. There was a garage and a toolshed, it looked like something you might find in a little village in the provinces somewhere, anywhere but in Paris. I remember we had dinner in the backyard, the daffodils were in bloom. Her family had been very kind to me, friendly and welcoming, and without treating me as special in any way, which made it even better. As her father was uncorking a bottle of Châteauneuf-du-Pape, it suddenly occurred to me that for the last twenty years Myriam had had dinner with her parents every night, that she helped her little brother with his homework, that she took her little sister shopping for clothes. They were a tribe, a close-knit family tribe, and as I thought back on my own life, it was so unlike anything I'd ever known that I almost broke down in sobs.

I hit MUTE. Marine Le Pen gestured more vigorously. She shook her fist, she threw open her arms. Obviously Myriam would go with her parents to Israel. There was nothing else she could do.

"I really hope I come back soon," she said, as if she'd read my mind. "I'm just going to wait a few months, till things calm down in France." I found her optimism slightly overdone, but I kept this to myself.

She stepped into her skirt. "With everything that's going on now, it's obvious the National Front's going to win. That's all we'll talk about at lunch. 'We told you so, sweetheart.' Still, they're good people, they only want what's best for me."

"Yes, they are good people. Truly good people."

"But what about you? What will you do? What do you think's going to happen at school?"

We were standing at the door. I realized that I hadn't the slightest idea, and also that I didn't give a fuck. I kissed her softly on the lips, and said, "There is no Israel for me." Not a deep thought, but that's how it was. She disappeared behind the elevator doors.

There followed an interval of, I suppose, several hours. The sun was setting between the apartment towers by the time I fully regained awareness of myself, of my circumstances, of everything. My mind had wandered in dark and troubled zones. I felt unutterably sad. Those sentences from *En ménage* kept coming back to me, piercing me, and I was painfully aware that I hadn't even suggested Myriam come live with me, that we move in together, but I knew that wasn't the real problem. Her parents were prepared to rent her an apartment, and mine was just a one-bedroom—a big one-bedroom, but still. Living together would have spelled the end of all sexual desire between us, and we were still too young to survive that as a couple.

In the old days, people lived as families, that is to say, they reproduced, slogged through a few more years, long enough to see their children reach adulthood, then went to meet their Maker. The reasonable thing nowadays was for people to wait until they were closer to fifty or sixty and then move in together, when the one thing their aging, aching bodies craved was a familiar touch, reassuring and chaste, and when the delights of regional cuisine, as celebrated every Sunday on *Les escapades de Petitrenaud*, took precedence over all other pleasures. For a while I sat there toying with the idea of writing an article for the *Journal of Nineteenth-Century Studies* in which I'd cite the proliferation of hit TV shows devoted to cooking, and in particular to regional cuisine, to argue that, after the long tyranny of modernity, Huysmans's clear-eyed conclusions had come around again, and were more relevant than ever. Then I realized that I no longer had the energy or desire to write an article, even for a publication as under the radar as the *Journal of Nineteenth-Century Studies*. I also realized, with a kind of incredulous stupefaction, that the TV was still on, still tuned to iTélé. I unmuted it: Marine Le Pen had given her speech hours ago, but all the pundits were still talking about it. She had called for a giant march on the Champs-Élysées. She had no intention of requesting a permit from the police, and if the authorities tried to interfere, she warned, the march would take place "by any means necessary." She'd concluded with a quotation from the Declaration of the Rights of Man and of the Citizen, the one from 1793: "When the government violates the rights of the people, insurrection is for the people, and for each portion of the people, the most sacred of rights and the most indispensable of duties." Naturally, the word *insurrection* had provoked a fair amount of comment. It even drew François Hollande out of his years of silence. At the end of his second disastrous administration—having been reelected only by pandering shamelessly to the National Front—the departing president had gone quiet, and the media seemed to have forgotten all about him. When he appeared on the steps of the Élysée, in front of the nine or ten journalists who showed up, and called himself the "last bastion of the republican order," there was brief but clearly audible laughter. Ten minutes later, the prime minister issued his own response. Purple-faced, veins bulging in his forehead, he looked apoplectic, and he warned that those who tested the limits of democratic legality would be dealt with as criminals. In the end, the only one who kept his cool was Ben Abbes: he defended the right of free assembly and challenged Le Pen to a debate on secularism—which the pundits generally agreed was a clever move, since it was nearly impossible for her to say yes. So he emerged, at no special cost to himself, as the voice of moderation and dialogue.

In the end I got bored and wound up flipping back and forth between reality shows on obesity, then I turned off the TV. The idea that political history could play any part in my own life was still disconcerting, and slightly repellent. All the same, I realized—I'd known for years—that the widening gap, now a chasm, between the people and those who claimed to speak for them, the politicians and journalists, would necessarily lead to a situation that was chaotic, violent, and unpredictable. For a long time France, like all the other countries of Western Europe, had been drifting toward civil war. That much was obvious. But until a few days before, I was still convinced that the vast majority of French people would always be resigned and apathetic—no doubt because I was more or less resigned and apathetic myself. I'd been wrong.

Myriam didn't call until Tuesday evening, a little past eleven; her voice was bright and full of confidence in the future. She was sure things in France would sort themselves out before long. I had my doubts. She'd even managed to persuade herself that Nicolas Sarkozy would return to politics, and be greeted as a savior. I didn't have the heart to disabuse her, but that struck me as improbable in the extreme. I had the sense that Sarkozy was finished with politics, that after 2017 he'd moved on.

Her flight was early the next morning, so there'd be no time to see each other before she left; she had so much to do—she had to pack, for starters. It wasn't easy to cram your whole life into thirty kilos of luggage. This was as I expected, but still I felt a pang as I hung up the phone. I knew that now I'd be truly alone.

Yet I felt almost cheerful the next morning as I rode the metro to class. The events of the last few days, even Myriam's leaving, seemed like a bad dream, a mistake that would be corrected soon enough. So I was taken aback when I got to the entrance of the building where class was held, in the rue de Santeuil, and found that the gate was locked. The guards normally opened up at 7:45. Several students, including a few I recognized as my second-years, stood waiting at the entrance.

It wasn't until almost eight thirty that a guard emerged from the administration building, stood in front of the gate, and informed us that the university was closed today, and would be closed until further notice. There was nothing more he could tell us, we should go home and wait to be "contacted individually." The guard was a black gentleman, Senegalese if I remembered right, whom I'd known for years and liked. As I was leaving, he took me by the arm and told me that, judging by the rumors among the staff, things were bad, really bad—he'd be extremely surprised if the university reopened anytime in the next few weeks.

•

Maybe Marie-Françoise would know what was going on. I tried to reach her several times that morning, without success. Around one thirty I gave up and turned on iTélé. A lot of protesters had already shown up for the National Front march. Place de la Concorde and the Tuileries were thronged. According to the organizers there were two million people—the police said three hundred thousand. Either way, I'd never seen such a crowd.

A giant, anvil-shaped cumulonimbus cloud hovered over the north of Paris, all the way from the Sacré-Coeur to the Opéra, its sides a dark, sooty gray. I looked over at the TV, where the huge crowd continued to gather, then I looked back at the sky. The storm cloud seemed to be moving slowly south. If it burst over the Tuileries, the demonstration would be seriously disrupted.

At exactly two o'clock, Marine Le Pen led the marchers down the Champs-Élysées toward the Arc de Triomphe, where she was scheduled to make a speech at three. I turned off the sound but went on looking at the screen. An immense banner stretched across the avenue, bearing the inscription "We Are the People of France." Many of the demonstrators had been given small placards that read, more simply, "This Is Our Home." That was the slogan they'd started using at extremist rallies—explicit, yet restrained in its hostility. The enormous cloud still hung there above the demonstration, motionless and

threatening. After a few minutes I got bored and went back
to *En rade*.

•

Marie-Françoise called a little after six; she didn't have much
news. The National Council of Universities had met the day
before, but no one was talking. In any case, she was sure
that the university wouldn't reopen till after the elections—
probably not until fall. The exams could always be given in
September. In general, the situation seemed serious. Her
husband was visibly worried. For the past week he'd been
spending fourteen-hour days at headquarters—he'd even
slept there the night before. Before we hung up, she promised to let me know if she heard any news.

There was nothing to eat at home, and I didn't want to
deal with the Géant Casino—after work was the wrong time
to go shopping in such a densely populated neighborhood—
but I was hungry. More than that, I felt like buying things to
eat, *blanquette de veau*, pollock with chervil, Berber-style
moussaka. Microwave dinners were reliably bland, but their
colorful, happy packaging represented real progress compared with the heavy tribulations of Huysmans's heroes.
There was no malice in them, and one's sense of participating
in a collective experience, disappointing but egalitarian,
smoothed the way to a partial acceptance.

The supermarket was strangely empty, and I filled my
cart fast, in a surge of enthusiasm mixed with fear. For some
reason, the word *curfew* crossed my mind. Some of the ca-
shiers, lined up behind their deserted checkout counters, were
listening to transistor radios. The protest was still going on,

so far without any incidents of violence. That would come later, I thought, once the crowd began to disperse.

The storm broke, violently, the moment I left the shopping center. Back at home I heated up some beef tongue in a Madeira reduction—rubbery, but edible—and turned on the TV. The fighting had begun. You could make out groups of masked men roaming around with assault rifles and automatic weapons. Windows had been broken, here and there cars were on fire, but the images, shot in the pelting rain, were of such poor quality it was impossible to get a clear idea of who was doing what.

III

I woke around four in the morning, lucid and alert. I took my time packing, assembling a small pharmacy and enough changes of clothing to last me a month. I even found the walking shoes—American, high-tech, never worn—that I'd bought a year before, when I thought I might take up hiking. I also packed my laptop, a stash of protein bars, an electric kettle, and instant coffee. By five thirty I was ready to go. I had no trouble starting the car or getting onto the Périphérique. By six o'clock I was almost in Rambouillet. I had no plan, no exact destination, just a very vague sense that I ought to head southwest—that if a civil war should break out in France, it would take a while to reach the southwest. I knew next to nothing about the southwest, really, only that it was a region where they ate duck confit, and duck confit struck me as incompatible with civil war. Though, of course, I could be wrong.

I didn't actually know much about France. After spending my childhood and adolescence in Maisons-Lafitte, a bourgeois suburb par excellence, I moved to Paris and never left. I had never really visited this country of which I was, somewhat theoretically, a citizen. It was something I'd always meant to do, hence the VW Touareg, which I bought around the same time I bought those hiking boots. It was a powerful car. With its turbo-diesel V-8 and 4.2-liter common-rail direct fuel injection, it could go 240 kilometers per hour. Although it was designed for highway driving, it also had real off-road capabilities. When I bought it, I must have been imagining weekend expeditions, long drives down country roads, but nothing like that ever took place. I was content to spend my Sundays browsing the rare book market in Parc Georges Brassens. And sometimes, I'm happy to say, I had spent my Sundays fucking—Myriam, mainly. My life would have been truly tedious and dreary if I hadn't, every now and then, fucked Myriam. I pulled over at a rest station called Mille Étangs—Thousand Ponds—right after the exit to Châteauroux. I bought a chocolate-chocolate-chip cookie and a large coffee at La Croissanterie, then I got back in the car to have my breakfast and think about the past, or nothing at all. The parking lot dominated the surrounding countryside, which was deserted except for a couple of cows—Charolais, probably. The sun was up now, but blankets of fog still drifted over the lower meadows. The landscape was rolling and quite beautiful, though there weren't any ponds—or brooks, for that matter. It seemed unwise to think about the future.

•

I turned on the car radio. The elections were off to a normal start; François Hollande had already voted in his "fiefdom" of Corrèze. Turnout, as far as anyone could tell this early in the day, was high, higher than in the last two presidential runoffs. Some pundits argued that a high turnout favored the "ruling party" against the challengers. Others, just as well regarded, thought the opposite. For the moment, in other words, nobody had any idea what the high turnout meant, and it was a little early for listening to the radio. I turned it off and pulled out of the lot.

Not long afterward, I saw I was low on gas—almost down to a quarter tank. I ought to have filled up at the rest station. I also noticed that the highway was strangely empty. Highways are never crowded on Sunday morning. That's the moment when society takes a deep breath and decongests, when its members give themselves the brief illusion of an individual existence. Even so, I'd driven a hundred kilometers without passing another car. The only vehicle I'd passed was a Bulgarian tractor-trailer weaving in and out of the emergency lane, drunk with fatigue. All was calm, I drove past striped, fluttering windsocks. The sun shone on the meadows and woods like a trusted employee. I turned the radio back on, but now it wasn't working: all my preprogrammed stations, from France Info to Europe 1, including Radio Monte-Carlo and RTL, were full of static. Something was happening in France, I knew it, and here I was, still driving along the hexagonal highway system at two hundred kilometers per hour—and maybe that was the solution. Everything in the country seemed to be broken, for all I knew the traffic radar was down, too. At the speed I was going, I'd reach the border at Jonquet by four. Things would be different in Spain, civil war slightly less imminent. It was worth a try. Except I was out of gas; yes, gas was at the top of the agenda. I kept my eye out for the next service station.

Which turned out to be the gas station at Pech-Montat. It had nothing special to recommend it on the information panel, no restaurant, no local crafts. This was a Jansenist station: its devotion to gas was pure. At first I was tempted to hold out for the Jardin des Causses du Lot, fifty kilometers south, but then I pulled myself together. I could always make a gas stop at Pech-Montat, then a pleasure stop at the Causses du Lot, where I'd load up on foie gras, Cabécou, and Cahors. I'd have them that very night in my hotel room on the Costa Brava. It was a plan—a sensible, manageable plan.

•

The parking lot was deserted, and right away I could tell something wasn't right. I slowed to a crawl before I pulled up, very carefully, to the service station. Someone had shattered the window, the asphalt was covered with shards of glass. I got out of the car and walked inside. Someone had also smashed the door of the refrigerated case where they kept the cold drinks and knocked over the newspaper dispensers. I discovered the cashier lying on the floor in a pool of blood, her arms clasped over her chest in a pathetic gesture of self-defense. The silence was total. I walked over to the gas pumps, but they were turned off. Thinking I might be able to find some way of turning them on behind the register, I went back into the shop and stepped reluctantly over the body, but I didn't see anything that looked like an ON switch. After a moment's hesitation, I helped myself to a tuna-vegetable sandwich from the sandwich shelf, a non-alcoholic beer, and a Michelin guide.

The closest of the local hotels recommended by Michelin was the Relais du Haut-Quercy, in Martel. All I had to do was get on the D840 and it was ten kilometers away. As I drove toward the exit, I thought I saw two bodies lying near the lot reserved for tractor-trailers. I got out of the car and went closer. Sure enough, two young North Africans, dressed in the typical uniform of the banlieues, had been shot down. There wasn't much blood, but it was obvious they were dead. One of them was still holding an automatic pistol in his hand. What could have happened? I tried the radio again, just in case, but still there was nothing—only the crackle of static.

•

Fifteen minutes later I'd reached Martel without incident. The road wound through a cheerful, wooded landscape. I didn't pass a single car, and I started to think I was going crazy, then I decided that everyone was staying home for exactly the same reason I'd left Paris: a premonition of imminent catastrophe.

The Relais du Haut-Quercy was a large white limestone building, two stories high, located just outside the village. The gate opened with a slight creak. I crossed the gravel courtyard and climbed the steps to the reception area. There was nobody there. Behind the counter, the room keys hung on their board. None of the keys was missing. I called out several times, each time louder than before, but no one answered. I went back outside. At the rear of the hotel was a terrace surrounded by rosebushes, with small round tables and wrought-iron chairs, where they must have served breakfast. I followed a broad path lined with chestnut trees for fifty meters or so before I came to a grassy esplanade with a view of the surrounding countryside. Deck chairs and umbrellas awaited hypothetical guests. For a few minutes I contemplated the landscape, rolling and peaceful, then I turned back toward the hotel. As I reached the terrace a woman came out, blond and fortyish, in a long gray woolen dress, her hair pulled back in a headband. She started when she saw me. "The restaurant is closed," she called out. I told her that I only wanted a room. "We don't serve breakfast, either," she elaborated. Only then did she admit, with obvious reluctance, that there was a room to be had.

She led me upstairs, opened a door, and handed me a tiny scrap of paper. "The gate locks at ten. After that, you have to use the code." She turned and left without another word.

Once I'd opened the blinds, the room wasn't so bad, except for the wallpaper, which was patterned with hunting scenes in dark magenta. I couldn't get the TV to work: there was no signal on any of the channels, just swarms of pixels. The Wi-Fi wasn't working, either. There were several networks that had names beginning with Bbox or SFR—those must have belonged to people in the village—but nothing that sounded like Relais du Haut-Quercy. I found an information sheet in a drawer. It listed various local attractions, there was also information on the local cuisine, but nothing about the Internet. Staying connected was obviously not a priority in this establishment.

After I'd unpacked, hung up the clothes I'd brought, plugged in my teakettle and my electric toothbrush, and turned on my phone to find no messages, I started to wonder what I was doing there. This very basic question can occur to anyone, anywhere, at any moment in his life, but there's no denying that the solitary traveler is especially vulnerable. If Myriam had been with me, I'd still have had no good reason for being in Martel, yet the question simply wouldn't have arisen. A couple is a world, autonomous and enclosed, that moves through the larger world essentially untouched; on my own, I was full of chips and cracks, and it took a certain amount of courage for me to slip the information sheet into my jacket pocket and go out into the village.

In the middle of Place des Consuls stood a grain market. It was clearly very old. I know almost nothing about architecture, but the houses on either side of it, built of a beautiful yellow stone, had to be a few centuries old at least. I'd seen things like that on TV, generally on shows hosted by Stéphane Bern, and these were just as good as the ones on TV, maybe better. One of the houses was really big, practically a palace, with groin-vaulted arcades and turrets, and when I went up close I learned that indeed the Hôtel de la Raymondie had been built between 1280 and 1350, and that it first belonged to the Vîcomtes de Turenne.

The rest of the village was more of the same. I walked down picturesque, deserted lanes until I reached the church of Saint-Maur. Massive, nearly windowless, it was a sort of ecclesiastical fortress. The information sheet said it had been built to resist the many attacks of the infidels who used to populate the region.

The D840, which crossed the village, continued on to Rocamadour. I had heard of Rocamadour, a well-known tourist destination with lots of Michelin stars. I even wondered whether I hadn't *seen* Rocamadour, on a Stéphane

Bern show. Still, it was twenty kilometers away. I opted for the smaller, winding road to Saint-Denis-les-Martel. After a hundred meters I happened on a tiny gatehouse made of painted wood where you could buy tickets for a tour of the Dordogne Valley by steam locomotive. That sounded interesting. It would be even better if you were a couple, I told myself with somber relish. Anyway, there was no one in the gatehouse. Myriam had been in Tel Aviv for several days now, enough time for her to find out about classes, maybe she'd already enrolled, or maybe she was spending her days at the beach. She loved the beach. We'd never gone on vacation together, I realized, I had never been good at choosing where to go or making reservations. I claimed to love Paris in August, but the truth was I was incapable of leaving.

A dirt path ran along the right-hand side of the railroad track. I followed it up the gentle slope of a thickly wooded hill and, after a kilometer, I found myself at a scenic overlook with an orientation table. A pictogram of a folding camera confirmed that this was, by vocation, a scenic overlook.

Below me flowed the Dordogne, encased between limestone cliffs some fifty meters high, obscurely pursuing its geological destiny. I learned from an information panel that the region had been inhabited since the dawn of prehistory. Cro-Magnon man had slowly driven the Neanderthals out of this valley. They had taken refuge in Spain, then disappeared.

I sat on the edge of the cliff, trying and failing to lose myself in the landscape. After half an hour, I took out my phone and called Myriam's number. She sounded startled to hear from me, but pleased. Everything was going well, she had a nice apartment with good light in the center of town.

No, she hadn't enrolled yet. How was I doing? Fine, I lied, but I missed her a lot. I made her promise to send me a very long e-mail, filling me in on everything, as soon as possible— forgetting that I couldn't get online.

I've always hated making kissing sounds on the phone. Even when I was young, I dreaded it, and forty years later it struck me as plainly ridiculous. I did it anyway. As soon as we hung up, I felt overwhelmed by a terrible loneliness, and I knew that I'd never have the courage to call Myriam again. The feeling of closeness when we talked on the phone was too violent, and the void that came afterward too cruel.

•

My attempt to interest myself in the natural beauty of the region was obviously doomed to failure, but I stuck it out a little longer, and night was falling as I made my way back to Martel. Cro-Magnon man hunted mammoth and reindeer; the man of today can choose between an Auchan and a Leclerc, both supermarkets located in Souillac. The only shops in the village were a bakery—closed—and a café on Place des Consuls, which also seemed to be closed. There were no tables set up on the square. Inside, though, I could see dim lights. I pushed the door open and went in.

Forty or fifty men were sitting in silence, watching a BBC News report on a TV hanging in the back of the room. No one turned to look when I walked in. They were locals, obviously, nearly all retirees, plus a few men who looked like manual laborers. I hadn't spoken English in a long time, and the presenter was talking too fast for me to really follow what he was saying. The others didn't seem to be doing much better than I was. The images, from various places—Mulhouse, Trappes, Stains, Aurillac—were of no obvious interest: community centers, nursery schools, empty gyms. It wasn't until they showed Manuel Valls, looking pale under the harsh lights on the steps of the Hôtel Marignon, that I began to reconstruct the events of the day: twenty polling stations, across France, had been attacked by groups of armed men early that afternoon. There had been no casualties, but the ballots had been stolen. So far, no one had claimed responsibility. Under the circumstances, the government had no choice but to suspend the elections. An emergency meeting had been called for later that evening, the president would take appropriate measures; the law of the Republic, he concluded rather flatly, would prevail.

I woke up around six to find the TV working again: the reception was bad on iTélé, but BFM was fine. Naturally, every program was devoted to the events of the day before. The pundits emphasized the extreme fragility of the democratic process: as a matter of electoral law, if even one polling station failed to report its results, anywhere in France, that invalidated the entire election. It was also emphasized that, until now, no group had ever thought of exploiting this weakness. Late in the night, the prime minister had announced that new elections would be held the following Sunday, this time with all polling stations under military protection.

As for the political implications, there was complete disagreement. I spent half the morning following the various contradictory arguments, then I took a book to the park. Huysmans's era had seen its own share of political strife. There had been the first anarchist attacks. There had been the anticlerical campaign of "Little Father" Combes—so much more violent than anything in our day—when the government actually seized church property and broke up congregations. This touched Huysmans personally: he was forced to leave his retreat at Ligugé Abbey, and yet he barely mentions it in his work. He seems never to have taken the slightest interest in politics at all.

I'd always loved the chapter in *À rebours* in which des Esseintes is inspired to plan a trip to London after rereading Dickens—then finds himself stuck in a tavern in the rue d'Amsterdam, unable to get up from the table. "An immense aversion to the voyage, an imperious need to remain calm washed over me . . ." At least I had managed to leave Paris, at least I'd made it as far as the Lot, I told myself as I contemplated the branches of the chestnuts lightly tossing in the breeze. I knew the hardest part was behind me: in the beginning, the solitary traveler meets with scorn, even hostility. Then, little by little, people get used to him, whether they're hoteliers or restaurateurs, and dismiss him as a harmless eccentric.

Sure enough, as I was heading back to my room around midday, the hotel manager greeted me with something like warmth and informed me that the restaurant would reopen that evening. New guests had arrived, an English couple in their sixties. The husband had the look of an intellectual, she intimated, maybe even a professor, the kind who insists on seeing the most out-of-the-way chapels and can tell you all about the Quercynois romanesque or the influence of the Moissac school. You never had any trouble from that sort of guest.

Like BFM, iTélé kept coming back to the political implications of the suspended elections. The top advisers of the

Socialist Party were meeting, the top advisers of the Muslim Brotherhood were meeting, even the top advisers of the UMP had decided they ought to hold a meeting. The newscasters, with their vans parked up and down along the rue de Solferino, the rue de Vaugirard, and the boulevard Malesherbes, more or less succeeded in hiding the fact that they had nothing of substance to report.

I went out around five o'clock: gradually, the village seemed to be coming back to life. The bakery was open. People were walking around in Place des Consuls. They looked pretty much the way I'd have imagined, if I'd tried to picture the inhabitants of a small village in the Lot. At the Café des Sports business was slow, and the curiosity about current events seemed to have been exhausted. The TV at the back of the room was tuned to Télé Monte-Carlo. I'd just finished my beer when I heard a familiar voice. I turned around: Alain Tanneur was at the cash register, paying for a box of Café Crème cigarillos. Under his arm was a paper bag from the bakery with a country loaf sticking out the top. Now Marie-Françoise's husband turned and saw me, too, his eyes a mask of surprise.

Later, over another beer, I explained to him that I was there by chance, and I told him what I'd seen at the gas station in Pech-Montat. He listened closely but without emotion. "I thought so," he said, once I'd finished my story. "I suspected that there had been unreported clashes, beyond the attacks on the polling stations. No doubt there were plenty of others across France."

He had good reason to be in Martel: he had a house there, which had belonged to his parents. He was a native, and soon he planned to retire and live there year-round. If the Muslim candidate won, Marie-Françoise was certain to lose her chair—obviously, no woman could hold a teaching position in an Islamic university. But what about his job at the DGSI? "They sent me packing," he said, with suppressed bitterness.

"I was fired Friday morning, me and my whole team," he went on. "They gave us two hours to clear out our desks."

"And do you know why?"

"I certainly do . . . On Thursday I submitted a report to my superiors warning them of possible incidents in different parts of the country—incidents meant to disrupt the elections. They did exactly nothing about it, and I was fired the next day." He let it sink in. "So? What conclusion would you draw?"

"You mean the government *wanted* it to happen?"

He gave a slow nod. "I couldn't prove it in court . . . because my report wasn't very precise. From what our informants were telling us, I was convinced that something would happen at or near Mulhouse, but I couldn't say for certain whether it would be polling station two, or five, or eight. To protect them all would have required a vast allocation of resources. It was the same for every threat. My superiors could always say that the DGSI had cried wolf before, and that the risk they took was reasonable. But as I say, I don't believe it."

"Do you know who was behind the attacks?"

"Who do you think."

"The nativists?"

"Yes, partly. And partly young jihadists—it was roughly half and half."

"These jihadists were working for the Muslim Brotherhood?"

"No." He shook his head firmly. "I've spent fifteen years of my life on this—and I've never found the slightest connection, or even any sign of contact, between the two groups. The jihadists are rogue Salafists. They may have resorted to violence, instead of prayer, but they're Salafists all the same. For them, France is a land of disbelief—Dar al-Kufr. For the Muslim Brotherhood, France is ready to be absorbed into the Dar al-Islam. More to the point, for the Salafists all authority comes from God. To them the very idea of popular representation is sacrilege. They'd never dream of founding, or supporting, a political party. Still, even if they're obsessed with global jihad, the young extremists do want Ben Abbes to win. They don't believe in him—for them, jihad is the one true path—but they won't stand in his way. It's exactly the same with the nativists. For them, civil war is the one true path, but some belonged to the National Front before they were radicalized. They'd never actively oppose it. From the beginning, both the National Front and the Muslim Brotherhood have chosen the way of the ballot. They've always wagered that they could take power *and* play by the rules of democracy. What's odd—even amusing, if you like—is that, a few days ago, each side decided that the other was about to win, that they had no choice but to disrupt the electoral process."

"Well, who do you think was right?"

"I haven't a clue." Now he relaxed and smiled. "There's a sort of legend, going back to the early aughts, that we have access to secret polls that never see the light of day. It's a fairy tale, partly. But it's also partly true, and the tradition has been kept up, to some degree. Well, in this case, our secret polls and the official polls show exactly the same results—fifty-fifty, give or take a few tenths of a percent."

•

I ordered another round. "You'll have to come over for dinner," Tanneur said. "Marie-Françoise will be so glad to see you. It's hard for her, having to leave the university. It doesn't make much difference to me—I'd have had to retire in two years anyway . . . Obviously, it leaves a bad taste, but they'll give me my whole pension, I'm sure, and extra pay, too. Anything to keep me from making a fuss."

The waiter brought our beers and a bowl of olives. The café had begun to fill up. People were talking loudly, it was clear they all knew one another, some said hello to Tanneur as they passed our table. I ate a couple of olives, thinking. There was something I didn't get. I could always just ask him, he might know, he seemed to know about lots of things. I regretted that until now my attention to political life had been so anecdotal, so superficial.

"What I don't understand," I said, after a sip of beer, "is what anyone hopes to achieve by attacking the polling stations. The elections are still going to take place, a week from now, under military protection. The balance of power hasn't changed. The results are still up in the air. Unless maybe they manage to prove that the right is behind it, which would help the Muslim Brotherhood—or that the Muslims are behind it, which would help the National Front."

"Trust me, no one can prove anything, one way or the

other—and no one's going to try. Politically, though, big things are going to happen. And fast. We'll see as soon as tomorrow. One possibility is that the UMP will decide to form a coalition with the National Front. So what, you say—the UMP are in free fall. Still, they're enough to tip the balance and win the election."

"I don't know. If they were going to ally themselves with the National Front, couldn't they have done it years ago?"

"Exactly right!" he beamed. "At the beginning, the National Front was eager to team up with the UMP so they could form a governing majority. Then, gradually, the National Front grew. Their numbers went up in the polls, and the UMP started to get scared. Not of their populism, or their supposed fascism—the leaders of the UMP wouldn't have minded a few new security measures, a little xenophobia. UMP voters, such as they are, are all for that sort of thing. But as a practical matter, the UMP is very much the weaker partner in this alliance. If they make a deal, they're afraid of being annihilated and simply absorbed into the National Front. And finally there's Europe. That's the deal killer. What the UMP wants, and the Socialists, too, is for France to disappear—to be integrated into a European federation. Obviously, this isn't popular with the voters, but for years the party leaders have managed to sweep it under the rug. If they formed an alliance with an openly anti-European party, they couldn't go on this way, the whole thing would fall apart. That's why I lean toward a second scenario, the creation of a republican alliance, where the UMP and the Socialists both get behind Ben Abbes—as long as they can get enough seats to form a government."

"I'd think that would be hard, too—or at least very surprising."

"Right again!" This time, as he smiled, he rubbed his hands together. Clearly, my questions amused him. "But it's hard for a different reason; it's hard *because* it's surprising, because nothing like it has ever happened—at least not since the Liberation. We're so used to the politics of right versus left that we can't see another way for things to be. And yet what's the problem, really? The UMP is much closer to the Muslim Brotherhood than the Socialists were. We talked about this the first time we met: the only reason that the Socialists gave way on education or reached a deal with the Brotherhood—the only reason their pro-immigrant wing won out over the secularists—is that they were cornered. They had no way out. It will all be much easier for the conservatives, who are in even worse shape, and who never cared about education—they hardly even know what education is. The only trouble is that the UMP and the Socialists would have to get used to the idea of governing together. That would be something completely new. It would undermine every position they've ever taken.

"Of course, there's a third possibility—that nothing will happen, no one will make a deal, and the runoff will take place with everyone in the same position as before, with the same uncertainty. In a sense, it's the most likely thing that could happen—but that's extremely worrisome, too. For one thing, no election has ever been so close in the entire history of the Fifth Republic. But what's really problematic is that neither of the leading parties has any experience of governing, at the national or even the local level. As politicians, they're all complete amateurs."

He finished his beer. When he looked at me his eyes glittered with intelligence. He wore a polo shirt under his glen plaid jacket; he was kindly, disillusioned, and wise; he probably subscribed to *Historia*. I could just see a dog-eared *Historia* collection in a bookcase by the fire, sandwiched between more specialized works, maybe about French Africa, or histories of the intelligence services since World War II. No doubt he'd been interviewed by the authors of these books, or soon would be, in his Quercynois retreat. On certain subjects he would remain silent, on others he would feel authorized to speak.

"So we'll see you tomorrow evening?" he asked, as he signaled for the check. "I'll pick you up at the hotel. Marie-Françoise will be delighted."

Evening fell on Place des Consuls, the yellow stones glowed gently in the setting sun. We were across from the Hôtel de la Raymondie.

"Martel is an old village, isn't it?"

"Very. And its name is no accident. Everyone knows Charles Martel—Charles the Hammer—fought the Arabs at Poitiers in 732, ending Muslim expansion to the north. That was a decisive battle, it marks the real beginning of the Christian Middle Ages. But it wasn't all so neat and tidy. The invaders didn't just pick up and go home. Charles Martel spent years warring against them in Acquitaine. In 743 he won another battle not far from here, and he decided to give thanks by building a church. It bore the three red hammers of his coat of arms. The village grew up around this church, which was later destroyed, then rebuilt in the fourteenth century. It's true that Christianity and Islam have been at war for a very long time; war has always been one of the major human activities. As Napoleon put it, war is human nature. But with Islam, I think, the time has come for accommodation, for an alliance."

I shook his hand goodbye. He was laying it on a little thick—the intelligence veteran, the old sage in retirement, etc., but after all he'd only just been fired. It would take him a while to grow into the part. In any case, I was already looking forward to dinner the next day. The port was bound to be good, and I had high hopes for the meal itself. He wasn't the type who took these things lightly.

"Watch the news tomorrow," he said before he walked away. "I suspect there will be something to see."

Sure enough, the news broke just after two in the afternoon. The center-right and the Socialists had formed a coalition, a "broad republican front," and were backing the Muslim Brotherhood. Frantic, the networks spent all afternoon asking about the terms of the deal and the division of ministries, and kept getting the same answer—about putting politics aside and unifying to bind the wounds of a divided nation, etc. All of which was predictable enough. More surprising was François Bayrou's return to the political stage. He had agreed to share the ticket with Ben Abbes: in return he would be named prime minister if Ben Abbes won.

These days the old mayor of Pau, who'd been beaten practically every time he ran for office over the last thirty years, was cultivating an image of *integrity*, with the connivance of various magazines. Which is to say, Bayrou was regularly photographed leaning on a shepherd's crook, wearing a beret—like Justin Bridou on the sausage labels—in a landscape of meadows and fields, usually in Labourd. The image he kept trying to promote, from interview to interview, was that of *the man who said no*, on the model of de Gaulle.

"It's genius, picking Bayrou—sheer genius," Alain Tanneur said the moment I showed up. He was literally quivering with enthusiasm. "I admit, it would never have occurred to me. This Ben Abbes really is something."

Marie-Françoise greeted me with a big smile. She wasn't just glad to see me, she was thriving. To see her bustling around the kitchen in an apron bearing the humorous phrase "Don't Holler at the Cook—That's the Boss's Job!" (or words to that effect), it was hard to believe that just days ago she'd been leading a doctoral seminar on the altogether unusual circumstances surrounding Balzac's corrections to the proofs of *Béatrix*. She'd made us tartlets stuffed with ducks' necks and shallots, and they were delicious. In his excitement, her husband uncorked a bottle of Cahors and one of Sauternes—then remembered his port, which I absolutely had to taste. On the face of it, I couldn't see what was so "genius" about bringing François Bayrou back into politics, but I was sure Tanneur would fill me in before long. Marie-Françoise gazed at him lovingly, clearly relieved that her husband was handling his dismissal so well, and adapting so easily to the role of armchair strategist—a role that would win him the admiration of the mayor, the doctor, the notary, and all the other notables still to be found in provincial towns. For them he'd always retain the glamour of a career in the secret services. The Tanneurs' retirement was off to a decidedly promising start.

"What's amazing about Bayrou, what makes him irreplaceable," Tanneur enthused, "is that he's an utter moron.

He's never had a political agenda beyond getting himself elected to the 'highest office in the land,' whatever that might take, and he's never had an idea of his own—he's never even pretended, which is unusual. If you're looking for a politician who can embody the humanist spirit, he's perfect: he thinks he's Henri the Fourth bringing peace through interfaith dialogue. Plus he plays well to the Catholic base, who find his stupidity reassuring. He's exactly what Ben Abbes needs, since he wants above all to embody a new humanism, and to present Islam as the best possible form of this new, unifying humanism—and by the way, he happens to mean it when he proclaims his respect for the three religions of the Book."

Marie-Françoise called us to the table. She'd made a salad of fava beans and dandelion with shaved Parmesan. It was so delicious that for a moment I lost the thread of the conversation. The Catholics had all but disappeared in France, her husband was saying, but they still enjoyed a certain moral authority. In any case, from the beginning Ben Abbes had done all he could to court them. Over the last year he'd paid no fewer than three visits to the Vatican. He appealed to the Third World types simply by being who he was, but he also knew how to win over conservative voters. Unlike his sometime rival Tariq Ramadan, who'd been tainted by his old Trotskyite connections, Ben Abbes had kept his distance from the anticapitalist left. He understood that the pro-growth right had won the "war of ideas," that young people today had become *entrepreneurs*, and that no one saw any alternative to the free market. But his real stroke of genius was to grasp that elections would no longer be about the economy but about values, and that here, too, the right was about to win the "war of ideas" without a fight. Whereas Ramadan presented sharia as forward-looking, even revolutionary, Ben Abbes restored its reassuring, traditional value—with a perfume of exoticism that made it all the more attractive. When he campaigned on family values, traditional morality, and, by extension, patriarchy, an avenue opened up to him that neither the conservatives nor the National Front could take without being called reactionaries or even fascists by the last of the *soixante-huitards*, those progressive mummified corpses—extinct in the wider world—who managed to hang on in the citadels of the media, still cursing the evil of the times and the *toxic atmosphere* of the country. Only Ben Abbes was spared. The left, paralyzed by his multicultural background, had never been able to fight him, or so much as mention his name.

Now Marie-Françoise served us a lamb shank confit with sautéed potatoes, and once again my attention began to wander. "Still, he is a Muslim," I murmured in my confusion.

"Yes, and so?" He was beaming. "He's a *moderate* Muslim. That's the point. He says so constantly, and it's true. You can't think of him as some kind of Taliban or terrorist. That would be completely mistaken. Ben Abbes has nothing but contempt for those people. You can hear it whenever he writes those editorials for *Le Monde*—underneath all the moral condemnation, there's an edge of contempt. In the end, he thinks of terrorists as amateurs. The reality is that Ben Abbes is an extremely crafty politician, the craftiest, most cunning politician France has known since François Mitterrand. And unlike Mitterrand he has a truly historic vision."

"So you think the Catholics have nothing to worry about?"

"Nothing to worry about? They have everything to gain! You know"—he smiled apologetically—"I've spent ten years on the Ben Abbes file. I can honestly say that only a few people in France know him better than I do. I've spent almost my whole career tracking Islamist movements. The first case I worked on—I was still a cadet at Saint-Cyr—was the Paris attacks in 1986, which we eventually traced back to Hezbollah and, indirectly, to the Iranians. Then there were the Algerians, the Kosovars, the al-Qaeda offshoots, the lone wolves . . . It's never stopped, in one form or another. So when the Muslim Brotherhood was created, we kept a close eye on them. It took us years to understand that, for all Ben Abbes's ambitions—and he's hugely ambitious—his plans had nothing to do with Islamic fundamentalism. There's an idea you hear in far-right circles, that if the Muslims came to power, Christians would be reduced to second-class citizens, or dhimmis. Now, dhimmitude is part of the general principles of Islam, it's true, but in practice the status of dhimmis is a very flexible thing. Islam exists all over the world. The way it's practiced in Saudi Arabia has nothing to do with the Islam you find in Indonesia or Morocco. In France, I promise you, they won't interfere with Christian worship—in fact, the government will increase spending for Catholic organizations and the upkeep of churches. And they'll be able to afford it, since the Gulf States will be giving so much more to the mosques. For these Muslims, the real enemy—the thing they fear and hate—isn't Catholicism. It's secularism. It's laicism. It's atheist materialism. They think of Catholics as fellow believers. Catholicism is a religion of the Book. Catholics are one step away from converting to Islam— that's the true, original Muslim vision of Christianity.

"What about the Jews?" The question slipped out—I hadn't planned on asking. The image of Myriam on my bed that last morning, in her T-shirt, with her little round ass, flashed through my mind. I poured myself another large glass of Cahors.

"Ah," he smiled again. "With the Jews, of course, things are somewhat more complicated. In theory, it's the same—Judaism is a religion of the Book, Abraham and Moses are recognized as prophets of Islam. In practice, though, relations with Jews in Muslim countries have often been more difficult than with Christians. And of course the Palestinian question has poisoned everything. Some small factions of the Muslim Brotherhood call for retaliation against the Jews, but I don't think they'll get anywhere. Ben Abbes has always maintained good relations with the Grand Rabbi of France. Every once in a while he may let the extremists act out, because even if he really hopes to convert Christians in massive numbers—and who says he won't?—he can't possibly have high hopes for the Jews. What would really make him happy, I think, is if they left France on their own and emigrated to Israel. In any case, I assure you, he'd never compromise his vast personal ambitions out of love for the Palestinians. It amazes me how few people have read his early writings—though, to be fair, they're all in obscure geopolitical journals. The first thing you notice is that he's always going on about the Roman Empire. For him, European integration is just a means to this glorious end. The main thrust of his foreign policy will be to shift Europe's center of gravity toward the south. There are already organizations pursuing this goal, like the Union for the Mediterranean.

The first countries likely to join up will be Turkey and Morocco, then later will come Tunisia and Algeria. In the long term, Egypt—that would be harder to swallow, but it would be definitive. At the same time, we'll see European institutions—which right now are anything but democratic—evolve toward more direct democracy. The logical outcome would be a president of Europe elected by the people of Europe. That's when the integration of populous countries with high birth rates, such as Turkey and Egypt, could be key. Ben Abbes's true ambition, I'm sure of it, is eventually to be elected president of Europe—greater Europe, including all the Mediterranean countries. Remember, he's only forty-three—even if he cultivates a paunch and refuses to dye his hair. In a sense, old Bat Ye'or wasn't wrong with her fantasy of a Eurabian plot. Her great mistake was in thinking the Euro-Mediterranean countries would be weak compared with the Gulf States. We'll be one of the world's great economic powers. The Gulf will have to deal with us as equals. It's a strange game Ben Abbes is playing with Saudi Arabia and the others. He's more than happy to accept their petro-dollars, but he won't give up the least bit of sovereignty in return. In a sense, all he wants is to realize de Gaulle's dream, of France as a great Arab power, and just you watch, he'll find plenty of allies—not least the petromonarchs, who have swallowed many a bitter pill for the Americans and alienated their own people in the process. They're starting to see that an ally like Europe, with fewer organic ties to Israel, might be a much better alternative . . ."

•

He fell silent; he'd been talking for half an hour straight. I wondered whether he was going to write a book, now that he was retired, and put his ideas down on paper. I thought his analysis was interesting—if you were interested in history, that is. Marie-Françoise brought in dessert: a *croustade landaise* with apples and nuts. It had been a long time since I'd eaten so well. After dinner, the thing to do would be to take a glass of Bas-Armagnac in the sitting room—and that's just what we did. Wilting in the brandy fumes, pondering the old spy's lustrous skull and plaid smoking jacket, I wondered what he really thought of all this. What opinion could a man have, after he'd spent his entire life clued in to the *inside story*? Probably none. I'd bet he didn't even vote—he knew too much.

"I went to work for French intelligence," he said, in a calmer tone, "partly, of course, because I'd spent my childhood fascinated by spy novels. But also, I like to think, it was because I'd inherited the patriotism that always impressed me in my father. He was born in 1922, if you can believe it. Exactly a hundred years ago. He joined the Resistance early on, in late June of 1940. Even in his day, French patriotism was an idea whose time had passed. You could say that it was born at the Battle of Valmy, in 1792, and that it began to die in 1917, in the trenches of Verdun. That's hardly more than a century—not long, if you think about it. Today, who believes in French patriotism? The National Front claims to, but their belief is so insecure, so desperate. The other parties have already decided that France should be dissolved into Europe. Ben Abbes believes in Europe, too, more than anyone, but in his case it's different. For him Europe is truly a project of civilization. Ultimately, he models himself on the emperor Augustus—and that's some model. We still have the speeches that Augustus made to the Senate, you know, and you can bet he has read them closely." He paused, then added, "It could be a great civilization, for all I know . . . Have you seen Rocamadour?" he asked all of a sudden. I was starting to nod off. I said no, I didn't think so—or rather yes, I'd seen it on TV.

"You must go—truly, you must. It's just twenty kilometers away, and it's one of the most famous shrines in the Christian world. Henry Plantagenet, Saint Dominique, Saint Bernard, Saint Louis, Louis the Eleventh, Philip the Fair—they all knelt at the foot of the Black Virgin, they all climbed the steps to her sanctuary on their knees, humbly praying that their sins be forgiven. At Rocamadour you'll see what a great civilization medieval Christendom really was."

•

Certain phrases of Huysmans about the Middle Ages floated vaguely through my mind. This Armagnac was absolutely delicious. I was about to answer Tanneur when I realized that I was incapable of expressing a coherent thought. To my great surprise, he began to recite Péguy in a firm and measured voice:

> *Happy are they who died for the carnal earth,*
> *So long as the war was just.*
> *Happy are they who died for four corners of earth.*
> *Happy are they who died a solemn death.*

It's hard to understand other people, to know what's hidden in their hearts, and without the assistance of alcohol it might never be done at all. To see this neat, elegant, cultured, ironic old man declaiming poetry surprised and moved me:

Happy are they who died in the great battles,
Who were laid upon the earth in the sight of God.
Happy are they who died on a last rampart
With all the trappings of great funerals.

He shook his head in resignation, almost in sadness. "You see, in the second stanza, to heighten the poem, Péguy has to bring in God. Patriotism alone isn't enough. He has to connect it with something stronger, to a higher mystery, and he makes the connection very clear in the next lines."

Happy are they who died for the carnal cities,
For these are the body of the city of God.
Happy are they who died for their hearths and fires
And the meager honors of their native homes.

For these are the image and the seed
And the body and the first taste of the house of God.
Happy are they who died in this embrace
Bound by honor and their earthly vows.

"The French Revolution, the republic, the motherland . . . yes, all that paved the way for something, something that lasted a little more than a century. The Christian Middle Ages lasted a millennium and more. Marie-Françoise tells me you're a specialist in Huysmans, but to my mind, no one grasped the soul of medieval Christianity as deeply as

Péguy—for all his republicanism, his secularism, his support of Dreyfus. And he understood that the true divinity of the Middle Ages, the beating heart of its devotion, wasn't God the Father, wasn't even Jesus Christ. It was the Virgin Mary. That, too, you can feel at Rocamadour."

•

I knew they were going back to Paris the next day, or the day after, to pack up for their move. Now that the "broad republican front" had formed its coalition, the results of the runoff were no longer in doubt, and neither was their retirement. After I sincerely congratulated Marie-Françoise on her culinary talents, I said goodbye to her husband at the door. He had drunk almost as much as I had, and still he could recite whole stanzas of Péguy by heart. I had to admit, I was impressed. I wasn't really convinced the republic and patriotism had "paved the way" for anything but a long succession of stupid wars, but in any case, Tanneur was far from senile. I wouldn't mind being that sharp when I was his age. At the bottom of the steps that led to the street, I turned and said, "I'll go to Rocamadour."

It wasn't peak tourist season yet, and I had no trouble booking a room at the Beau Site Hotel, agreeably located within the medieval citadel. The restaurant offered a view of the Alzou: the site was, in fact, impressive and received plenty of visitors. After a few days watching wave after wave of tourists from all four corners of the earth, each tourist different, each the same, camcorder in hand, roaming amazed over the jumble of towers, parapets, oratories, and chapels that climbed the side of the cliff, I felt as if I had somehow stepped out of historical time, and I barely noticed when, on the evening of the second electoral Sunday, Mohammed Ben Abbes won by a landslide. I had drifted into a dreamy state of inaction, and even though here the hotel Internet worked fine, I wasn't especially worried not to have heard from Myriam. In the eyes of the owner and his staff, I was a type: a bachelor, rather cultured, rather sad, without much in the way of distractions—all accurate enough. In the end, I was the kind of guest who never gives you any trouble, which was all that mattered.

I'd been at Rocamadour for a week or two when finally I got her e-mail. She had lots to say about Israel, about the special atmosphere she felt all around her—extraordinarily dynamic and lively, but with an undercurrent of tragedy. It might seem strange, she wrote, to leave a country like France because you were afraid of hypothetical dangers, only to emigrate to a country where the dangers weren't the least bit hypothetical. A Hamas splinter group had just launched a new series of attacks, and practically every day some bomb-wearing kamikaze blew himself up in a restaurant or on a bus. It was strange, but now that she was there she understood: since Israel had always been at war, the attacks and the battles seemed inevitable, in a sense natural. They didn't keep people from enjoying life, at any rate. She attached two photos of herself in a bikini on the beach in Tel Aviv. In one of the photos, a three-quarters rear view of her running toward the sea, you could really see her ass and I started to get a hard-on; I wanted to touch her ass so badly my hands tingled with pain. It was incredible how well I remembered it.

Closing up my computer, I realized that she hadn't once said anything about coming back to France.

•

Early in my stay I fell into the habit of visiting the Chapel of Our Lady. Every day I went and sat for a few minutes before the Black Virgin—the same one who for a thousand years inspired so many pilgrimages, before whom so many saints and kings had knelt. It was a strange statue. It bore witness to a vanished universe. The Virgin sat rigidly erect; her head, with its closed eyes, so distant that it seemed extraterrestrial, was crowned by a diadem. The baby Jesus—who looked nothing like a baby, more like an adult or even an old man—sat on her lap, equally erect; his eyes were closed, too, his face sharp, wise, and powerful, and he wore a crown of his own. There was no tenderness, no maternal abandon in their postures. This was not the baby Jesus; this was already the king of the world. His serenity and the impression he gave of spiritual power—of intangible energy—were almost terrifying.

This superhuman image was a world away from the tortured, suffering Christ of Matthias Grünewald, which had made such a deep impression on Huysmans. For Huysmans the Middle Ages meant the Gothic period, really the late Gothic: emotionally expressive, realistic, moralizing, it was already closer to the Renaissance than to the Romanesque. I remembered a conversation I'd had, years before, with a history professor at the Sorbonne. In the early Middle Ages, he'd explained, the question of individual judgment barely came up. Only much later, with Hieronymus Bosch, for example, do we see those terrifying images in which Christ separates the cohort of the chosen from the legion of the damned; where devils lead unrepentant sinners toward the torments of hell. The Romanesque vision was much more communal: at his death the believer fell into a deep sleep and was laid in the earth. When all the prophecies had been fulfilled and Christ came again, it was the entire Christian people who rose together from the tomb, resurrected in one glorious body, to make their way to paradise. Moral judgment, individual judgment, individuality itself, were not clear ideas in the mind of Romanesque man, and I felt my own individuality dissolving the longer I sat in my reverie before the Virgin of Rocamadour.

Still, I had to get back to Paris. One morning it hit me that it was already the middle of July, and that I'd been there for more than a month. The truth was, I had no pressing reason to go back. I'd received an e-mail from Marie-Françoise, who'd been in touch with other colleagues: no news from the administration. We were all in limbo. In the larger world, the legislative elections had been held, with predictable results, and a government had been formed.

The town began to hold organized events for the tourists. Mainly these were gastronomical, but some were cultural, and the day before I left, as I made my usual visit to the Chapel of Our Lady, I happened on a reading of Péguy. I sat in the next-to-last row; attendance was sparse. Most of the audience was made up of young people in jeans and polo shirts, all with those open, friendly faces that for whatever reason you see on young Catholics:

Mother, behold your sons who fought so long.
Weigh them not as one weighs a spirit,
But judge them as you would judge an outcast
Who steals his way home along forgotten paths.

The alexandrines rang out rhythmically in the stillness, and I wondered what the patriotic, violent-souled Péguy could mean to these young Catholic humanitarians. In any case, the actor had excellent diction. I thought that he must be a well-known theater actor, a member of the Comédie Française, but that he must also have been in the movies, because I'd seen his photo somewhere before.

Mother, behold your sons and their numberless ranks.
Judge them not by their misery alone.
May God place beside them a handful of earth
So lost to them, and that they loved so much.

He was a Polish actor, I was sure of it now, but still I couldn't think of his name. Maybe he was Catholic, too. Some actors are. It's true that they practice a strange profession, in which the idea of divine intervention seems more plausible than in some other lines of work. As for these young Catholics, did they love their homeland? Were they ready to give up everything for their country? I felt ready to give up everything, not really for my country, but *in general*. I was in a strange state. It seemed the Virgin was rising from her pedestal and growing in the air. The baby Jesus seemed ready to detach himself from her, and it seemed to me that all he had to do was raise his right hand and the pagans and idolators would be destroyed, and the keys to the world restored to him, "as its lord, its possessor, and its master."

Mother, behold your sons so lost to themselves.
Judge them not on a base intrigue
But welcome them back like the Prodigal Son.
Let them return to outstretched arms.

Or maybe I was just hungry. I'd forgotten to eat the day before, and possibly what I should do was go back to my hotel and sit down to a few duck's legs instead of falling down between the pews in an attack of mystical hypoglycemia. I thought again of Huysmans, of the sufferings and doubts of his conversion, and of his desperate desire to be part of a religion.

•

I stayed until the reading ended, but once it was over I realized that, despite the great beauty of the text, I'd have preferred to spend my last visit alone. What this severe statue expressed was not attachment to a homeland, to a country; not some celebration of the soldier's manly courage; not even a child's desire for his mother. It was something mysterious, priestly, and royal that surpassed Péguy's understanding, to say nothing of Huysmans's. The next morning, after I filled up my car and paid at the hotel, I went back to the Chapel of Our Lady, which now was deserted. The Virgin waited in the shadows, calm and timeless. She had sovereignty, she had power, but little by little I felt myself losing touch, I felt her moving away from me in space and across the centuries while I sat there in my pew, shriveled and puny. After half an hour, I got up, fully deserted by the Spirit, reduced to my damaged, perishable body, and I sadly descended the stairs that led to the parking lot.

IV

As I returned to Paris, as I crossed the toll gate at Saint-Arnoult, as I passed Savigny-sur-Orge, Antony, then Montrouge, as I turned off for the exit at Porte d'Italie, I knew that what lay before me was a joyless but not an empty life. It would be filled with minor assaults. As I'd expected, someone had taken advantage of my absence to steal the parking space that came with my apartment, and there was a trickle of water underneath the refrigerator. These were the only domestic incidents. My mailbox was full of various kinds of bureaucratic mail, some of which would require an immediate response. To maintain order in your bureaucratic life, you more or less have to stay home; go away for any length of time and you're always likely to run afoul of some agency or other. I knew it would take several days to get back up to speed. I performed some summary triage, throwing away the least interesting ads, keeping the targeted offers (the "three-day madness" at Office Depot, the private sale at Cobrason), then I gazed out at the uniformly gray sky.

I spent a few hours gazing out the window, now and then refilling my glass of rum, before I attacked the letters. The first two, from my insurance company, informed me that it was impossible to fulfill certain requests for reimbursement and invited me to send a new request with photocopies of the appropriate documents attached. This was the kind of mail I was used to, and generally left unanswered. The third letter, by contrast, held a surprise. Sent from the city hall in Nevers, it expressed its deepest condolences on the death of my mother and informed me that the body had been transported to the city coroner's office, which I should contact in order to make the necessary arrangements. The letter was dated Tuesday, May 31. I quickly flipped through the pile. There was a follow-up letter postmarked June 14 and another from June 28. Finally, on July 11 the city informed me that, pursuant to article L 2223–27 of the General Local Authorities Code, the city had deposited my mother's body in the common division of the municipal cemetery. I had five years to order the exhumation of her body and its reburial in a private plot, at the end of which time it would be cremated and the ashes scattered in a "garden of memory." If I were to request this exhumation, I would be liable for the expense incurred by the municipality—one coffin, four bearers, the cost of the plot itself.

I certainly hadn't imagined my mother leading a vibrant social life, attending conferences on pre-Columbian civilization or making the rounds of the local Romanesque churches with other women her age. Even so, I had no idea she was so completely alone. They'd probably tried to get in touch with my father, too, and he must have left the letters unanswered. In spite of everything, it bothered me to think of her being buried in a potter's field (this, the Internet informed me, was the former name for the common division of the municipal cemetery), and I wondered what had become of her French bulldog (humane society? euthanasia by injection?).

Next I set aside the payment-due notices and the other bills. Those were easy. All I had to do was put each one in the appropriate file in order to isolate the correspondence with my two essential interlocutors, those pillars of a man's life: my health insurer and the tax bureau. I didn't have the courage to face that right away, and I decided to have a look around Paris—well, maybe not Paris, that would be too much on my first day back. I'd start off with a stroll around the neighborhood.

As I pushed the elevator button, it occurred to me that I hadn't received any mail from the university. I went back and checked my bank statements: my paycheck had been direct-deposited, as usual, at the end of June. My job status was just as uncertain as ever.

•

The change in the political regime had left no visible mark on the neighborhood. Tight knots of Chinese men still gathered in front of the OTB, racing forms in hand. Others hurried along pushing handcarts full of rice noodles, soy sauce, mangos. Nothing, not even a Muslim government, could curb their incessant activity—Muslim proselytizing would dissolve without a trace, like the Christian message before it, in the vast ocean of their civilization.

I wandered through Chinatown for an hour or more.

The parish of Saint-Hippolyte was still offering its introductory courses in Mandarin, and there were the flyers for the "Asian Fever" club nights in Maisons-Alfort. I couldn't find any visible signs of change other than the disappearance of the kosher section from the Géant Casino. Mass retail was nothing if not opportunistic.

Things were different in Italie 2. As I'd predicted, the Jennyfer store had disappeared, replaced by a kind of organic Provençal boutique offering essential oils, olive oil, and honey harvested from the garrigue. Less explicably, no doubt for strictly economic reasons, the L'Homme Moderne franchise, located in a more or less dead zone of the second floor, had also closed its doors. It had yet to be replaced. The biggest change, a subtle one, was in the shoppers themselves. Like all shopping centers—though naturally, in a much less spectacular way than those in La Défense or Les Halles—Italie 2 had always attracted a fair amount of riff-raff. They'd completely disappeared. Also, women's clothing had been transformed. I felt the change at once, but I couldn't put it into words. The number of Muslim veils had increased only slightly—it wasn't that. I spent almost an hour walking around before it hit me: all the women were wearing pants. To visualize a woman's thighs and to mentally reconstruct her pussy where the thighs intersect—a process whose power of excitation is directly proportional to the length of bare leg—was so involuntary and mechanical with me, so genetic you might say, that it took me a while to notice what was missing: no more dresses or skirts. Women were wearing a new garment, a kind of long cotton smock, ending at mid-thigh, which eliminated any objective interest in the tight pants that some women might potentially wear; as for shorts, these were obviously out of the question. The contemplation of women's asses, that small, dreamy consolation, had also become impossible. A transformation was indeed under way. There'd been a fundamental shift. Several hours of channel surfing revealed no further changes, but then soft-core porn had gone out of fashion years before.

It was two weeks before I received the letter from Paris III. According to the new statutes of the Islamic University of Paris–Sorbonne, I was no longer permitted to teach. Robert Rediger, the new president of the university, had signed the letter himself. He expressed his profound regret and assured me that this was no reflection on the quality of my scholarship. I was, of course, welcome to pursue my career in a secular university. If, however, I preferred to retire, the Islamic University of Paris–Sorbonne could offer me a pension, effective immediately, at a starting monthly rate of 3,472 euros, to be adjusted for inflation. I was invited to schedule a meeting with HR in order to fill out the necessary paperwork.

I reread the letter three times in disbelief. It was, practically to the euro, what I'd have gotten if I had retired at sixty-five, at the end of a full career. They really were willing to pay to avoid any trouble. No doubt they had overestimated the ability of academics to make a nuisance of themselves. It had been years since an academic title gained you access to major media, under rubrics such as "tribune" or "points of view"; nowadays these had become a private club. Even if all the university teachers in France had risen up in protest, almost nobody would have noticed, but apparently they hadn't found that out in Saudi Arabia. They still believed, deep down, in the power of the intellectual elite. It was almost touching.

•

From outside, nothing about the university looked different, except for the gilded star and crescent above the doors, next to the big inscription "Université Sorbonne Nouvelle–Paris III." Inside the administrative buildings, the transformations were more visible. In the waiting room, one was welcomed by a photograph of pilgrims making their way around the Kaaba, and the offices were decorated with posters bearing hand-lettered verses from the Koran. The secretaries had changed, I didn't recognize any of them, and they all wore veils. One of them gave me a pension application. Its simplicity was disconcerting. I filled it out right there, on the corner of a table, signed it, and gave it back. As I walked out into the courtyard, I realized that my academic career had just ended in a matter of minutes.

When I got to the Censier metro I stopped at the top of the stairs, not knowing what to do. I couldn't go straight home as if nothing had happened. The stalls of the Mouffetard market had just opened. I was wandering along the edges of the charcuterie d'Auvergne, contemplating the flavored saucissons (blue cheese, pistachio, hazelnut) without really seeing them, when I spotted Steve coming up the street. He saw me at the same time, and it looked as if he wanted to avoid me, but it was too late, I was already walking toward him.

As I expected, he had accepted a position at the new university: he was teaching a course on Rimbaud. He clearly found the situation embarrassing, and he added, unprompted, that the new administration hadn't interfered at all with the content of his course. That is to say, Rimbaud's conversion to Islam was presented as a matter of historical fact—though this was controversial, to say the least—but when it came to analyzing the poems, he really had been left alone, and that's what counted. The longer I listened without any sign of indignation, the more he relaxed, and in the end he invited me for coffee.

"It took me a long time to make up my mind," he said, once he'd ordered a Muscadet. I nodded, full of warmth and understanding; I figured it had taken him ten minutes, tops. "But the salary was pretty attractive . . ."

"Even the pension isn't bad."

"The salary's a lot better."

"How much better?"

"Three times more."

•

Ten thousand euros a month for a mediocre teacher no one had ever heard of who couldn't produce a paper worthy of the name—they really did have deep pockets. Oxford had slipped through their fingers; the Qataris had swooped in at the last minute with a higher bid, so they'd decided to double down on the Sorbonne. They'd even bought up apartments in the Fifth and Sixth Arondissements for faculty housing.

He'd been given a very attractive two-bedroom in the rue du Dragon for next to nothing.

"I think they really wanted to keep you," he added, "but they didn't know where you were. To be honest, they actually asked me to help them track you down; I had to tell them I only saw you at work."

A few minutes later, he walked me to the metro. Just as I was about to enter the station, I asked, "What about the girls?" He grinned. "Obviously, that's all changed. I guess you could say things are organized differently now. I got married," he added, rather brusquely. Then he elaborated: "To one of my students."

"They arranged that for you, too?"

"Not exactly. Let's just say they don't discourage the possibilities of contact with female students. I'm getting another wife next month." With that he headed off toward the rue de Mirbel, leaving me openmouthed at the top of the stairs.

I stood there for several minutes and then finally decided to go home. When I reached the platform, I saw that the next train to Mairie d'Ivry was leaving in seven minutes. A train pulled into the station, but it was going to Villejuif.

I was *in my prime*. I didn't suffer from any lethal illness. The health problems that regularly assailed me were painful, but they were minor. I had a good thirty or even forty years before I reached that dark zone where all illnesses are basically fatal, where nearly every illness entails an *end-of-life* discussion. I had no friends, that was true, but when did I ever? Besides, if you really thought about it, what was the point of having friends? Once you reach a certain stage of physical decline, the only relationship that really, clearly makes sense is marriage (the bodies blend together, to a degree, and produce a new organism, at least if you believe Plato). That stage was well on its way. I had maybe ten years, probably less, before the decline grew visible and I could no longer be described as *still young*. As for my marital prospects, clearly I was off to a bad start. Over the passing weeks, Myriam's e-mails had become more infrequent, and shorter. Lately she had given up the salutation "Dearest" and replaced it with a neutral "François." It was only a matter of weeks, I thought, before she, too, would announce that she had *met someone*.

The meeting had already taken place, that much I knew. I don't know exactly how I knew, but something in her choice of words, in the diminishing number of her smiley faces and hearts, left no room for doubt. She just didn't have the courage to tell me. She was pulling away from me, it was as simple as that. She was making a new life for herself in Israel—what did I expect? She was a lovely girl, intelligent and kind, extremely attractive. Yes, what did I expect? For Israel, at any rate, she showed the same unflagging enthusiasm. "It's hard, but I know why I'm here," she wrote. Obviously, that was more than I could say for myself.

Although it took a few weeks to sink in, the end of my academic career had deprived me of all contact with female students. What was I supposed to do? Sign on to a dating site like Meetic, as so many had done before me? I was a man of culture. I had a certain status. As I've said, I was *in my prime*; and if, after several weeks of strained conversation, in which one or two bursts of enthusiasm on whatever subject—say, Beethoven's late quartets—covered up my growing, generalized ennui and held out the promise of magical moments or of a complicity based on shared wonder and laughter; if after several weeks I actually met up with one of my numerous female analogues, what would come of it? Erectile dysfunction on one side, vaginal dryness on the other. I'd just as soon give it a pass.

I had made only very occasional forays onto escort sites, usually during the summer months as a sort of stopgap between one student and the next. A quick glance online was enough to assure me that these sites were alive and well under the new Islamic regime. I spent a few weeks going back and forth, examining the different profiles, printing out certain ones so I could reread them. (Escort sites were something like restaurant guides, whose remarkable flights of lyricism evoked pleasures decidedly superior to the dishes one actually tasted.) Eventually I decided on Nadia, a girl of Tunisian extraction. It was arousing, in a way, to pick a Muslim, given the overall political situation.

But Nadia, I learned, had been altogether untouched by her generation's overwhelming return to Islam. The daughter of a radiologist, she'd lived in good neighborhoods since she was a girl and had never considered wearing the veil. She was doing her master's degree in literature—she could have been one of my old students, but no, she was at Paris-Diderot. Sexually, she was conscientious, but she assumed each new position like a robot. You could tell she wasn't really there. She only perked up, vaguely, when we got to sodomy. She had a tight little ass, but for some reason I didn't experience any pleasure, I felt as if I could spend hours fucking it without the slightest fatigue or joy. As she started to whimper, it seemed to me that she was afraid of enjoying herself, as if it might lead to actual feelings. She quickly turned around and finished me off in her mouth.

Before I left, we sat and talked for a few more minutes on her folding sofa, long enough to use up the hour I'd paid for. She was intelligent, but altogether conventional. Whether we were discussing the election of Ben Abbes or Third World debt, her opinions were all the generally approved ones. Her studio was tasteful and impeccably furnished. I could tell she behaved sensibly, that far from spending what she made on expensive clothes, she put most of it aside. Indeed, she confirmed that in just four years—she'd started when she was eighteen—she had made enough to buy the studio where she worked. She planned to keep at it long enough to complete her studies, then she was thinking of a career in broadcasting.

A few days later I went to see Slutty Babeth, whose site was full of enthusiastic testimonials, and who described herself as "hot and up for anything." Indeed, she welcomed me into her pretty, slightly old-fashioned one-bedroom wearing nothing but a cut-out bra and a crotchless thong. She had long blond hair and an open, almost angelic face. She, too, had a taste for sodomy, but she didn't try to hide it. After an hour, I still hadn't come, and she remarked that I was really resistant. It was the same as before: even though I never lost my erection, I never experienced any pleasure, either. She asked me to come on her breasts; I did. Spreading the semen over her chest, she told me that she loved to be covered in cum. She was a regular participant in gang bangs, usually held in swingers' clubs, sometimes in parking lots or other public places. Although she charged a nominal fee—fifty euros per person—she made a lot at these parties, since she invited as many as forty or fifty men, who took turns in all three orifices before they came on her. She promised to let me know next time she organized a gang bang. I thanked her. The truth was, I wasn't interested, but she seemed like a nice person.

All of which is to say, these two escorts were *fine*. Still, that wasn't enough to make me want to see them or have sex with them again, or to make me go on living. Should I just die? The decision struck me as premature.

•

In the event, it was my father who died, a few weeks later. I got the news over the phone from Sylvia, his partner. She said she was sorry that we hadn't "had much chance to talk." This was a euphemism: in fact, we'd never spoken at all. I had learned of her existence only two years before, the last time my father and I had talked, when he'd happened to mention her in passing.

She came to pick me up at the Briançon train station. The trip had been very unpleasant. The high-speed train to Grenoble still ran all right, they maintained basic service on the TGV, but the TER was falling apart. The train to Briançon broke down more than once. We ended up arriving an hour and fifteen minutes late. The toilets were stopped up, a puddle of water and shit had overflowed into the corridor and threatened to spread into the compartments.

Sylvia was behind the wheel of a Mitsubishi Pajero Instyle, and to my utter stupefaction the seats were covered in fake leopard skin. The Mitsubishi Pajero (I learned from the special issue of *Auto-Journal* that I bought when I got home) is "one of the best recreational vehicles for handling back-country roads." The Instyle model comes with leather upholstery, electric sunroof, back-up camera, and an 860-watt, twenty-two-speaker Rockford Acoustic audio system. The whole thing left me profoundly shaken, since my father had always—at least, as long as I knew anything about him— been so rigidly, almost affectedly bourgeois in his good taste. He wore the three-piece suits (gray chalk stripe or occasionally dark blue) and the expensive English ties of a successful CFO, which is exactly what he was. With his wavy blond hair, sky-blue eyes, and handsome face, he could have appeared in one of those movies that Hollywood makes every few years about some abstruse but supposedly important issue to do with finance, subprimes, and Wall Street.

I hadn't seen him in six years, and had no idea how his life might have changed, but nothing could have prepared me for his metamorphosis into a suburban adventurer.

Sylvia was fiftyish, about twenty-five years his junior. If not for me, everything would have gone to her. My existence meant that she would be deprived of my portion of the estate—50 percent, since I was an only child. Under the circumstances, one could hardly expect her to feel any warmth toward me, but she behaved reasonably well and addressed me without excessive hostility. I'd called several times to let her know the train was running late, and the lawyer had pushed our appointment back to six o'clock.

The reading of my father's will held no big surprises: he had divided his estate between us equally, with no additional bequests. Still, the lawyer had done his job. He began by itemizing my father's holdings.

My father had received a generous pension from Unilever but had very little in cash: two thousand euros in his checking account, some ten thousand that he'd invested in a mutual fund a long time ago and probably forgotten. His main asset was the house where he and Sylvia lived: a broker in Briançon had appraised it at 410,000 euros. His Mitsubishi, almost new, was selling for 45,000 euros online. The one surprising thing was his collection of high-priced guns, which the lawyer listed according to their value: the most expensive were a Verney-Carron Platines and a Chapuis Oural Élite. Altogether, the collection was worth 87,000 euros—a good deal more than the SUV.

"He collected guns?" I asked Sylvia.

"They weren't collector's pieces. He did a lot of hunting. It had become his great passion."

An ex-CFO of Unilever buying an off-road SUV and discovering his inner hunter-gatherer—it was surprising, but I could see it. The lawyer had already finished; the division would be dismayingly simple. The proceedings were swift, but I still missed my train, thanks to the earlier delay. It was the last train that evening. This placed Sylvia in an awkward position, as we both realized, probably at the same moment, when we got back in the car. I was quick to let her off the hook. I said the best thing for me, by far, was to find a hotel near the station. There was a very early train I had to catch, I told her, because I had an extremely important meeting in Paris. I was lying on both counts: not only did I not have a meeting the next day, but the earliest train didn't leave until noon. The earliest I could hope to be back in Paris was six o'clock. Reassured that I was about to vanish from her life, she was almost enthusiastic in her offer of a drink at "our house," as she persisted in calling it. Not only was it no longer "their" house, now that my father was dead, but soon it wouldn't be hers, either. Given the state of her finances, as I understood them, there was no way she could give me my share of the inheritance without selling the place.

•

Their chalet, which overlooked the Freissinières Valley, was enormous. The underground garage could have held ten cars. Crossing the hallway into the living room, I paused in front of a cluster of stuffed trophies, chamois or mouflons—at any rate, that kind of mammal. There was also a wild boar. That one I recognized.

"Take off your coat, if you like," Sylvia said. "Hunting is

nice, you know—I hadn't known anything about it, either. They'd go hunting every Sunday, all day, then we'd have dinner together with the other hunters and their wives, all twenty of us. We'd have everyone over for a drink, and often, afterward, we'd go to a little restaurant with a private room, in the next village."

•

So my father's last years had been *nice*. This, too, was a surprise. When I was growing up, I'd never met anyone he worked with, and I don't think he ever saw anyone—outside of work, that is. Had my parents had any friends? If so, none that I remembered. We had a big house in Maisons-Lafitte—not as big as this one, certainly, but big. I didn't remember anyone ever coming to dinner or spending the weekend, or doing any of the things people do with their *friends*. What's worse, I don't think my father ever had what you'd call a *mistress*, either. I couldn't be sure, of course, I didn't have any proof, but I just couldn't connect the idea of a mistress with the man I remembered. In other words, he had led two entirely separate lives, one having nothing to do with the other.

The living room was vast. It must have taken up the entire floor, if you included the open-plan kitchen (on the right, as you walked in) and the farmhouse table beside it. The rest of the space was filled with coffee tables and deep white leather sofas, with more hunting trophies on the wall and a rack for my father's guns. They were beautiful objects, and their elaborate metal inlays shone with a gentle glow. The floor was strewn with various animal skins—mainly sheep, I'd guess. It was kind of like being in a German porn flick from the seventies, set in a Tyrolean hunting lodge. I went over to the picture window. It took up the whole back wall and looked out on the mountains. "Across from us," Sylvia said, "you can see the top of La Meije. And to the north there's the Barre des Écrins. Can I offer you a drink?"

I'd never seen such a well-stocked bar. There were ten different kinds of brandy, plus certain liqueurs I had never even heard of, but I asked for a martini. Sylvia turned on a lamp. Nightfall cast a bluish tinge over the snow-covered mountains, and sadness settled over the room. Even without my inheritance, I couldn't imagine that she would want to live alone in a house like this. She still worked, she did something in Briançon, I didn't know what. She'd told me on our way to the lawyer's office, but I'd forgotten. Obviously, even if she moved into a nice apartment in the center of Briançon, her life was going to be much less pleasant than before. I sat down somewhat reluctantly on the sofa and accepted another martini, but I'd already decided that it would be my last. When I finished this one I'd ask her to drive me to the hotel. It was becoming more and more obvious to me that I would never understand women. Here was a normal— almost cartoonishly normal—woman, and yet she'd seen something in my father, something my mother and I never saw. And I don't think it was only, or even mainly, a question of money. She made plenty herself; that much was clear from her clothes, her hair, the way she talked. In that ordinary old man she, and she alone, had found something to love.

When I got back to Paris there was the e-mail I'd been dreading for the last few weeks. Or no, that's not quite true, I think I was already resigned to it. What I really wanted to know was whether Myriam, too, would tell me that she had *met someone*—whether she'd use the expression.

She used the expression. In the next paragraph she said she was deeply sorry, and that she'd never think of me without a certain sadness. I believed that was true—and also true that she wouldn't think of me very often. Then she changed the subject, pretending to be consumed with worry over the political situation in France. That was kind, her acting as if somehow we'd been torn apart by the whirlwind of history. It wasn't entirely honest, of course, but it was kind.

I turned away from the computer screen and went over to the window. A single lenticular cloud, its edges tinted orange by the setting sun, hovered high above the Charléty stadium, as immobile and indifferent as an intergalactic spaceship. I felt a dull, numb pain, that's all, but it was enough to keep me from thinking clearly. All I knew was that once again I found myself alone, with even less desire to live and nothing to look forward to but aggravations. Quitting the university had been extremely simple, whereas dealing with my social security and health insurer turned out to be a huge bureaucratic undertaking, one that I didn't have the courage to face. And yet I had to. Even my very comfortable pension wouldn't be enough to see me through a serious illness. On the other hand, it did allow me to sign up for more escorts. I felt no real desire, only an obscure Kantian notion of "duty toward the self," as I surfed my usual sites. In the end I settled on an ad posted by two girls: a twenty-two-year-old Moroccan named Rachida and a twenty-four-year-old Spaniard named Luisa promised "the enchantments of a wild and mischievous duo." They were expensive, obviously, but I thought I was entitled to a little extravagance, all things considered. We made a date for that same evening.

At first everything went the way it usually did, which is to say, fine. They had a nice studio near Place Monge. They'd lit incense and put on soft music, whale songs or something. I penetrated them and fucked them in the ass, one after the other, without fatigue or pleasure. It was only after half an hour, when I was taking Luisa from behind, that I felt the stirrings of something new. Rachida kissed me on the cheek, then with a little smile she slipped behind me. She rested one hand on my ass, then leaned in and started licking my balls. Little by little, with growing amazement, I felt shivers of forgotten pleasure. Maybe Myriam's e-mail, and the fact that she'd, as it were, officially left me, freed me up in some way. I don't know. Wild with gratitude, I turned around, tore off the condom, and offered myself up to Rachida's mouth. Two minutes later, I came between her lips. She meticulously licked up the last drops as I stroked her hair.

Before I left, I insisted on tipping them a hundred euros each. Maybe it was too soon to give up after all—witness these two girls, and my father's surprising late-life transformation. And maybe, if I kept seeing Rachida on a regular basis, we'd end up having feelings for each other. At least, there was no reason to absolutely rule it out.

This brief surge of hope came during the most optimistic moment that France had known since the Thirty Glorious Years half a century before. The first days of Ben Abbes's national unity coalition had been a unanimous success. All the pundits agreed that no newly elected president had ever enjoyed such a "state of grace." I thought often of what Tanneur had told me about the new president's international ambitions, and although it went practically unnoticed, I was intrigued to see that Morocco had reentered negotiations to join the EU. There was already a timetable in place for Turkey. The rebuilding of the Roman Empire was well under way, and in his domestic policies Ben Abbes had gone from strength to strength. His first achievement was a dramatic drop in crime: in the most troubled neighborhoods it was down 90 percent. He'd had another instant success with unemployment, which had plummeted. This was clearly due to women leaving the workforce en masse—due, in turn, to the highly symbolic first measure passed by the new government: a large new subsidy for families. At first there had been some squirming on the left, since the subsidy was reserved for women who gave up working. The new unemployment figures put an end to that. The subsidy hadn't even added to the deficit, since it was completely offset by drastic cuts in education—until now, far and away the largest item in the national budget. Under the new system, mandatory education ended with elementary school, around age twelve. For most children, the school certificate would be their last degree. From then on, vocational training was encouraged. Secondary and higher education had been completely privatized. All of these reforms were meant to "restore the centrality, the dignity, of the family as the building block of society": so the new president and his prime minister declared in a strange joint speech during which Ben Abbes reached nearly mystical heights, while François Bayrou, his face wreathed in a beatific smile, more or less played the role of John Sausage, the Hanswurst of old German folk plays, who repeated—in an exaggerated, slightly grotesque way—everything the main character said. Muslim schools were doing fine, obviously. When it came to education, the Gulf States still had plenty to spend. More surprisingly, some Catholic and Jewish schools seemed to have made the best of a bad situation by appealing to various CEOs. In any case, they announced that they had covered their costs and would open as usual in the fall.

At first the brutal implosion of the two-party system, which had ruled French politics since time immemorial, plunged the media into a stupor bordering on aphasia. You could see poor Christophe Barbier trailing from one news set to the next, his scarf at half-mast, seemingly unable to comment on a historic change that he hadn't seen coming. The truth was nobody had. And yet, as the weeks went by, nodes of opposition began to form—first, on the antireligious left. Protests were organized by the rather unlikely team of Jean-Luc Melenchon and Michel Onfray. The Left Front still existed, at least on paper, and it was clear that Ben Abbes would face a challenge in 2027, and not just from the National Front. On the other side, groups like the Union of Salafist Students rose up to denounce the persistence of immorality and demand sharia law. So, little by little, the stage was set for a political debate. This would be a new kind of debate, unlike anything in recent French history, more like what existed in the Middle East. But still it would be a debate, of a sort. And the existence of political debate, however factitious, is necessary to the smooth functioning of the media—and, perhaps also, to keep people feeling that they live, at least technically, in a democracy.

Beneath these surface agitations, France was undergoing deep and rapid change. It turned out that some of Ben Abbes's ideas had nothing to do with Islam: during a press conference he declared (to general bafflement) that he was profoundly influenced by distributism. He had actually said so before, several times, on the campaign trail, but since journalists have a natural tendency to ignore what they don't understand, no one had paid attention and he'd let it drop. Now that he was a sitting president, the reporters were forced to do their homework. So, over the next few weeks, the public learned that distributism was an English economic theory espoused at the turn of the last century by G. K. Chesterton and Hilaire Belloc. It was meant as a "third way," neither capitalism nor communism—a sort of state capitalism, if you like. Its central idea was to do away with the separation between capital and labor. For distributists, the basic economic unit was the family business; when in certain sectors consolidation became necessary, the government had to ensure that the workers remained the owners and managers of their own enterprise.

Distributism, Ben Abbes later explained, was perfectly compatible with the teachings of Islam. This was not self-evident, since Chesterton and Belloc were known during their lifetimes as outspoken Catholic polemicists. It soon became clear that although their doctrine was avowedly anticapitalist, Brussels wouldn't have much to worry about. The main practical measures adopted by the new government were, on the one hand, to end state subsidies for big business—which Brussels had always fought in the name of free trade—and, on the other, to adopt policies that favored craftsmen and small-business owners. These measures were an instant hit: for decades, every young professional in the country had dreamed of starting his own business, or at least of becoming his own boss. The measures also reflected changes in the national economy: despite the costly efforts to save heavy industry in France, factories continued to close, one after the other, so farmers and craftsmen managed to compete and even, as they say, to grow their market share.

These developments were turning France into a new kind of society, but it took a young sociologist, Daniel Da Silva, to articulate the change. His groundbreaking essay was ironically entitled "One Day, Son, All This Will Be

Yours." The subtitle was more straightforward: "Toward a Reason-Based Family." In the introduction, Da Silva expressed his debt to an essay by the philosopher Pascal Bruckner, published a decade earlier, in which Bruckner had argued that marriage for love was a failure; he called for a return to marriage based on reason. Da Silva maintained that family ties, especially the tie between father and son, cannot be based on love, only on the transmission of practical knowledge and on inheritance. The transition to a salaried workforce had doomed the nuclear family and led to the complete at-omization of society, and society could be rebuilt only if industry was based on a small-business model. In the past, arguments against romance may have enjoyed a succès de scandale, but before Da Silva the media never took them seriously, thanks to the universal consensus concerning individual liberty, the mystery of love, and so on. Da Silva was quick on his feet, an excellent debater, and basically in-different to political or religious ideology. By sticking to his area of expertise—the evolution of family structures and their effects on the birthrate in Western societies—he kept from being swallowed up by his right-wing admirers, and instead became a leader in the debates that had begun to form (albeit very slowly, very gradually, without great animus, in a general atmosphere of tacit and lazy acceptance) around the domestic policies of Mohammed Ben Abbes.

My own family history was a perfect illustration of Da Silva's arguments. As for love, it had never seemed more remote. The miracle of my first visit to Rachida and Luisa had failed to produce a sequel, and once more my dick had become an organ as efficient as it was unfeeling. I left their studio in a state of near despair, knowing that I would probably never see them again, and that my viable options were slipping ever more quickly through my fingers, leaving me, as Huysmans would have put it, "unmoved and dry."

Not long after, a cold front several thousand kilometers long approached Western Europe. After stagnating for a few days over the British Isles, the polar air mass swept across France overnight, bringing unseasonably low temperatures.

My body, no longer a source of pleasure, retained its capacity for suffering, and within a few days I realized that, for maybe the tenth time in three years, I'd fallen victim to dyshidrosis. Tiny pustules spread across the soles of my feet and between my toes, merging to form one oozing, raw mass. At the dermatologist's office I was told that the rash had been aggravated by an opportunistic fungal infection. It was treatable, but the treatment took a long time, and I shouldn't expect to see any improvement for several weeks. In the meantime, I woke up every night in pain. I had to scratch for hours, until I bled, to get any relief. I couldn't believe that my toes, those plump, absurd little pieces of flesh, could be ravaged by such piercing torments.

•

One night, after one of these orgies of scratching, I got up and walked, bleeding, to the bay window. It was three in the morning, but as always in Paris, the sky wasn't completely dark. From my window I could see ten high-rises, a few hundred medium-size buildings. A few thousand apartments in all, a few thousand *households*—which by now tended to mean two people or, more and more often, just one. Most of the cells were dark. I had no more reason to kill myself than most of these people did. On reflection, maybe even less. My life was marked by real intellectual achievements. In a certain milieu—granted, a very small one—I was known and even respected. Financially, I had nothing to complain about. Until I died I was guaranteed a generous income, twice the national average, without having to do any work. And yet I knew I was close to suicide, not out of despair or even any special sadness, simply from the degradation of "the set of functions that resist death," in Bichat's famous formulation. The mere will to live was clearly no match for the pains and aggravations that punctuate the life of the average Western man. I was incapable of living for myself, and who else did I have to live for? Humanity didn't interest me—it disgusted me, actually. I didn't think of human beings as my brothers, especially not when I looked at some particular subset of human beings, such as the French, or my former colleagues. And yet, in an unpleasant way, I couldn't help seeing that these human beings were just like me, and it was this very resemblance that made me avoid them. I should have found a woman to marry. That was the classic, time-honored solution. A woman is human, obviously, but she represents a slightly different kind of humanity. She gives life a certain perfume of exoticism. Huysmans would have posed the problem in almost exactly the same terms. Not much had changed since then, except in an incidental and negative way, through slow erosion and leveling—but no doubt even this leveling, these changes, had been greatly exaggerated. In the end Huysmans had taken another path, he had chosen the more radical exoticism of *religion*; but that path still left me just as perplexed as the other.

•

A few more months went by. My dyshidrosis eventually went away, but it was replaced almost immediately by an extremely violent outbreak of hemorrhoids. The weather grew colder and colder, my movements more and more predictable: one outing per week to the Géant Casino, for stocking up on food and for conversation, and a daily outing to the mailbox to collect the books I ordered on Amazon.

Even so, I got through the holidays without excessive despair. The year before, I had still received a few Happy

New Year e-mails—from Alice, in particular, and a few university colleagues. This year, for the first time, nobody wrote.

The night of January 19, I burst into unexpected tears and couldn't stop crying. In the morning, as dawn rose over Le Kremlin-Bicêtre, I decided to return to Ligugé Abbey, where Huysmans had taken his monastic vows.

The TGV to Poitiers was delayed indefinitely, the announcement said, and railroad security guards fanned out over the platforms so that no one would be tempted to light a cigarette. The trip was beginning badly, in other words, and new inconveniences awaited me on the train. The luggage area was even smaller than it had been the last time I took the TGV. It was now practically nonexistent. Suitcases and bags lay piled up in the corridors, so that moving from one car to another—previously the main attraction of travel by rail—was difficult and soon became impossible. The Servair café car, which took me twenty-five minutes to get to, held more disappointment: short as the menu was, most of the items were unavailable. The national rail service and Servair apologized for any inconvenience. I had to settle for a quinoa salad with balsamic dressing and an Italian sparkling water. At the station I'd bought a *Libération*, more or less in desperation. One of the articles ended up catching my eye around the time we reached Saint-Pierre-des-Corps. Apparently, this distribution of the new president's wasn't as harmless as everyone had thought. One pillar of Chesterton and Belloc's philosophy was the principle of subsidiarity: that no entity (social, financial, or political) could take charge of any function if it could be handled by a smaller entity. Pope Pius XI defined the principle in his encyclical *Quadragesimo Anno*: "Just as it is wrong to withdraw from the individual and to commit to the community at large what private enterprise and endeavor can accomplish, so it is likewise unjust and a gravely harmful disturbance of right order to turn over to a greater society of higher rank functions and services which can be performed by lesser bodies on a lower plane." In this case, the function newly considered a "disturbance of right order" was the welfare state. What could be more beautiful, Ben Abbes enthused in his latest speech, than to see welfare where it belonged, in the warm setting of the nuclear family. At the time, the "warm setting of the nuclear family" was still mainly a *program*, but in concrete terms, the new budget projected an 85 percent reduction in welfare benefits over the next three years.

The really surprising thing was that he'd lost none of his hypnotic magic. Even now, his projects met with no serious opposition. The left had always been able to make cuts in social spending that the right never could, but this was even more true of the Muslim party. In the international pages, I saw that the negotiations to bring Algeria and Tunisia into the EU were proceeding apace, and that by the end of the year both countries would, with Morocco, become European states. Preliminary talks had begun with Lebanon and Egypt.

•

Things started to look up when we got to Poitiers. There were plenty of taxis, and the driver didn't blink when I asked him to take me to Ligugé Abbey. He was middle-aged and heavyset, with soft, thoughtful eyes. He drove his Toyota subcompact very carefully. Every week, he told me, people came from all over the world to stay there, in the oldest Christian monastery in the West. Just last week he'd driven a famous American actor—he couldn't think of his name, but he knew he'd seen him in the movies. (A brief inquiry established that the person he had in mind was probably, although not certainly, Brad Pitt.) He trusted that I would have a very pleasant stay: it was so peaceful, and the meals were delicious. As he said it, I realized that he was expressing not just a belief, but a hope, because he was one of those people, and you don't see them every day, who take an instinctive pleasure in the happiness of their fellow men—that he was, in other words, *a nice guy*.

•

Off to the left of the entrance hall was the monastery shop, where you could buy monastic handicrafts—but the shop was closed right now, and there was no one at the reception desk to the right. A small sign instructed visitors to ring for assistance, but asked that they refrain during the daily offices, except in case of emergency. There was a timetable, but it didn't say how long the offices lasted. After a fairly lengthy calculation involving mealtimes, I concluded that for everything to fit in one day, each office probably couldn't take longer than half an hour. A shorter calculation revealed that right then we were somewhere between Sext and None, so I could ring.

A few minutes later, a tall monk appeared wearing a black habit. His face lit up when he saw me. He had a high fore-head, dark brown curly hair with hardly any gray, and a dark brown beard. He couldn't have been a day over fifty. "I'm Brother Joel," he said, and hefted my bag. "I'll take you to your room." He stood up very straight and carried my bag easily, although it was heavy. Clearly, he was in excellent shape. "It's good to have you back," he went on. "It's been more than twenty years, hasn't it?" I must have looked con-fused. "Didn't you stay with us twenty years ago?" he asked. "You were writing about Huysmans?" It was true, but I was amazed that he remembered me. I had no memory of him at all.

"You're what they call the guest master, aren't you?"

"No, no—but I was then. That job tends to be given to the younger monks, or I should say, the ones who are new to monastic life. The guest master speaks to our guests, he's still in contact with the world. It's like a sort of airlock, or a halfway step, before the monk takes the plunge into his vocation of silence. I did it for a little more than a year."

We were walking alongside a quite beautiful Renaissance building, surrounded by a park. A dazzling winter sun spar-kled down on the tree-lined paths, which were strewn with dead leaves. A church stood in the distance, slightly taller than the cloister, late Gothic in style. "That's our old church, the one Huysmans knew," said Brother Joel. "But our com-munity was dispersed by the Combes laws at the turn of the century, and when we finally managed to reassemble, we couldn't get the church back, only the cloister buildings. We had to build a new church inside the monastery itself." We stopped in front of a small one-story building in the same Renaissance style. "Here's our guesthouse," he was saying, when all at once a sturdy monk, maybe forty years old and wearing the same black habit, came hurrying down the path. A vigorous man, with a head so bald it practically gleamed in the sun, he projected extreme serenity and competence. He called to mind a finance minister—he even looked a bit liked Pierre Moscovici—or better yet a budget minister, someone, in any case, who inspired automatic and limitless trust. "And here is Brother Pierre, our new guest master. He'll be handling all the logistics of your visit. I just came to welcome you back." He bowed, shook my hand, and walked off toward the cloister.

"You came on the TGV," asked the guest master; I said I had. "It's fast, all right, the TGV," he went on, clearly hoping to start us off on a basis of mutual agreement. Then, taking my bag, he led me to my room. It was roughly three meters square, hung with light gray, textured wallpaper. The carpeting was medium gray and threadbare. The only decoration was a large crucifix of dark wood hanging above a small single bed. I immediately noticed that the sink had separate taps for hot and cold, and that there was a smoke detector on the ceiling. I told Brother Pierre that the room would be just fine, but I already knew that wasn't true. In *En route*, when Huysmans debates—more or less interminably—whether he can stand monastic life, one of his negative arguments is that, apparently, they wouldn't let him smoke indoors. Moments like that have always made me love him. There's another passage where he writes that one of the few pure joys in life is getting into bed with a stack of good books and a packet of tobacco. Huysmans never had to deal with smoke detectors.

There was a fairly rickety wooden desk with a Bible on it, a thin tract by Dom Jean-Pierre Longeat on the meaning of a monastic retreat (it was stamped "Do Not Remove"), and an information sheet that basically just listed the schedule of offices and meals. I saw at a glance that it was almost time for None, but I decided to give it a pass, this first day: the symbolism was less than thrilling. The idea behind the offices of Terce, Sext, and None was to "return us to the presence of God over the course of the day." Every day there were seven offices, plus Mass. None of that had changed since Huysmans's time. The one concession to comfort was that Vigils, which had been observed at two in the morning, was now at ten p.m. During my first visit, I had loved Vigils, with the long meditative psalms chanted in the middle of the night—as distant from Compline, and its farewell to the day, as it was from Lauds, which greeted the new dawn. Vigils was an office of pure waiting, of ultimate hope without any reason for hope. Obviously, in the dead of winter, back when the church wasn't even heated, it can't have been easy.

What impressed me most was that Brother Joel had recognized me after more than twenty years. Not much must have happened in his life since he stopped being guest master. He had worked in the monastery workshops, done the daily offices. His life had been peaceful, and probably happy, in stark contrast to my own.

I went for a long walk in the park, smoking numerous cigarettes, as I waited for Vespers, which was what came before the evening meal. The sun grew more and more dazzling. It made the frost sparkle, casting a yellow glow over the buildings, a scarlet glow over the carpet of dead leaves. I no longer knew the meaning of my presence in this place. For a moment it would appear to me, weakly, then just as soon it would disappear. In any case, it clearly had little to do with Huysmans anymore.

Over the next two days I got used to the litany of prayers, but I never actually managed to love them. Mass was a recognizable element, the one point of contact with religious devotion as we in the outside world might know it. The rest was a matter of reading and chanting the appropriate psalms according to the time of day. Sometimes these were interspersed with a brief sacred text, read aloud by one of the monks—readings also occurred at meals, which were taken in silence. The modern church, constructed within the monastery walls, had a sober ugliness to it. Architecturally, it was reminiscent of the Super-Passy shopping center in the rue de l'Annonciation, and its stained-glass windows, simple patches of abstract color, weren't worth looking at, but none of that bothered me. I wasn't an aesthete—I had infinitely less aesthetic sense than Huysmans—and for me the uniform ugliness of contemporary religious art was essentially a matter of indifference. The voices of the monks rose up in the freezing air, pure, humble, well meaning. They were full of sweetness, hope, and expectation. The Lord Jesus would return, was about to return, and already the warmth of his presence filled their souls with joy. This was the one real theme of their chants, chants of sweet and organic expectation. That old queer Nietzsche had it right: Christianity was, at the end of the day, a feminine religion.

All of this might have suited me fine, but going back to my cell ruined it: the smoke detector glared at me with its little red hostile eye. Sometimes I went and smoked out the window, so I could confirm that here, too, things had gone downhill since Huysmans's day: the TGV tracks lay just beyond the far edge of the monastery grounds, two hundred meters away as the crow flies. The trains went by at full speed, and their roar shattered the meditative silence several times an hour, every hour. But the cold grew more intense, and after each of these stations at the window I had to warm myself against the radiator for minutes at a time. My mood soured, and the prose of Dom Jean-Pierre Longeat—no doubt an excellent monk, full of love and good intentions—exasperated me more and more. "Life should be a continual loving exchange, in tribulations or in joy," the good father wrote. "So make the most of these few days and exercise your capacity to love and be loved, in word and deed." "Give it a rest, dipshit," I'd snarl, "I'm alone in my room." "You are here to lay down your burdens and take a journey within yourself, to the wellspring where the power of desire is revealed." "My only fucking desire is to have a fucking cigarette," I raged, "I've reached the fucking wellspring, dipshit, and that's what's there." I may not have had, like Huysmans, "a heart hardened and smoked dry by dissipation," but lungs hardened and smoked dry by tobacco—those I had.

"Hear, taste, and drink, weep and chant, knock at the

door of Love!" exclaimed the ecstatic Longeat. On the morning of the third day I realized I had to leave. The whole thing had been a mistake from the beginning. I explained to Brother Pierre that, to my dismay, unforeseen professional obligations, of literally unbelievable importance, required me to cut my spiritual journey short. With that Pierre Moscovici face of his, I knew he'd believe me. He might even have *been* Pierre Moscovici, in his previous life, and the Pierre Moscovicis of the world are an understanding bunch. I was sure we'd get through this without any unpleasantness. As we were saying goodbye in the entrance hall, he expressed a hope that my journey among them had been a journey in the light. Not to worry, I assured him, I'd had a terrific time. And yet, at that moment, I felt that I was somehow letting him down.

During the night, a low-pressure system, originating over the Atlantic, had moved in from the southwest. The temperature had risen by six degrees; the countryside around Poitiers was wrapped in fog. I had called ahead for a taxi, and now I found myself with almost an hour to kill. I spent it at the Bar de l'Amitié, whose front door was fifty meters from the monastery, mindlessly downing Leffes and Hoegaardens. The waitress was thin and wore too much makeup. The other customers were talking in loud voices, mainly about real estate and vacations. It gave me no satisfaction to be back among people like myself.

V

If Islam is not political, it is nothing.

—Ayatollah Khomeini

At the Poitiers train station, I had to change my ticket. The next TGV to Paris was almost full, so I paid for the upgrade to Pro Première. According to the national rail service, it was a universe of privilege, with a guaranteed high-speed connection, larger tables for spreading out work papers, and electrical outlets so that you'd never find your laptop dying on you because you'd stupidly forgotten to charge it; otherwise, it was normal first class.

•

I found a seat by myself, with no one across from me. On the other side of the aisle a middle-aged Arab businessman, dressed in a long white djellaba and a white keffiyeh, had spread out several files on the two tables in front of his seat. He must have been coming from Bordeaux. There were two young girls facing him, barely out of their teens—his wives, clearly—who had raided the newsstand for candy and magazines. They were excited and giggly. They wore long robes and multicolored veils. For the moment, one was absorbed in a *Picsou* comic, the other in the latest issue of *Oops.*

Across from them, the businessman looked as if he was under some serious stress. Opening his e-mail, he downloaded an attachment containing several Excel spreadsheets, and after examining these documents, he looked even more worried than before. He made a call on his cell phone. A long, hushed conversation ensued. It was impossible to tell what he was talking about, and I tried, without a great deal of enthusiasm, to get back to my *Figaro*, which covered the new regime from a real estate and luxury angle. From this point of view, the future was looking extremely bright. The subjects of the petromonarchies were more and more eager to pick up a pied-à-terre in Paris or on the Côte d'Azur, now that they knew they were dealing with a friendly country, and were outbidding the Chinese and the Russians. Business was good.

Peals of laughter: the two young Arab girls were hunched over the copy of *Picsou*, playing "Spot the Difference." Looking up from his spreadsheet, the businessman gave them a pained smile of reproach. They smiled back and went on playing, now in excited whispers. He took out his cell again and another conversation ensued, just as long and confidential as the first. Under an Islamic regime, women— at least the ones pretty enough to attract a rich husband— were able to remain children nearly their entire lives. No sooner had they put childhood behind them than they became mothers and were plunged back into a world of childish things. Their children grew up, then they became grandmothers, and so their lives went by. There were just a few years where they bought sexy underwear, exchanging the games of the nursery for those of the bedroom—which turned out to be much the same thing. Obviously they had no autonomy, but as they say in English, *fuck autonomy*. I had to admit, I'd had no trouble giving up all of my professional and intellectual responsibilities, it was actually a relief, and I had no desire whatsoever to be that businessman sitting on the other side of our Pro Première compartment, whose face grew more and more ashen the longer he talked on the phone, and who was obviously in some kind of deep shit. Our train had just passed Saint-Pierre-des-Corps. At least he'd have the consolation of two graceful, charming wives to distract him from the anxieties facing the exhausted businessman—and maybe he had two more wives waiting for him in Paris. If I remembered right, according to sharia law you could have up to four. What had my father had? My mother, that neurotic bitch. I shuddered at the thought. Well, she was dead now. They were both dead. I might have seen better days, but I was the only living witness to their love.

It was warmer in Paris, too, but not as warm. A fine cold rain was falling on the city. Traffic was bad on the rue Tolbiac, which struck me as strangely long. I thought I had never seen a street so long, so dreary, dull, and endless. I wasn't expecting to come home to anything in particular, just various headaches. And yet, to my surprise, there was a letter in my mailbox—or at least something that wasn't junk mail, or a bill, or a bureaucratic request for information. I glanced at my living room in disgust, unable to pretend that I felt any special pleasure at coming home to this apartment where no one was loved, this apartment that nobody loved. I poured myself a large Calvados and then I opened the letter.

It was signed by Bastien Lacoue, who had apparently replaced Hugues Pradier as head of Éditions de Pléiade a few years before. I hadn't known anything about that. He began by saying that, thanks to some inexplicable oversight, Huysmans was not yet in the Pléiade catalog, although he obviously belonged to the canon of classic French literature; as to that, I could only agree. He went on to express his conviction that, given my universally recognized contributions to the field, there was no one to whom the Pléiade could better entrust the editing of Huysmans's work than me.

It was an offer I couldn't refuse. Or rather, I could refuse, obviously, but it would mean renouncing all intellectual and social ambition—all ambition, period. Was I really ready for that? There was no way I could think it over without a second Calvados. After thinking it over, I decided that the really prudent thing was to go out and buy another bottle.

•

Just two days later, I found myself meeting with Bastien Lacoue. His office was exactly the way I'd imagined it, old-fashioned, up three flights of steep wooden stairs, overlooking a disheveled courtyard. Lacoue himself was a modern-day intellectual with frameless little oval glasses, a jovial man. He radiated satisfaction with himself, the world, and his position in it.

I'd done some preparation, and told him that I thought Huysmans's works should be divided into two volumes, the first containing everything from *Le drageoir à épices* through *La retraite de Monsieur Bougram* (I held 1888 to be the most likely year of composition), the second devoted to the Durtal novels, from *Là-bas* through *L'oblat*, and of course *Les foules de Lourdes.* This division was simple, logical, even obvious, and without hidden complications. As always, the real question was how to handle the notes. Certain pseudo-scholarly editions had seen fit to provide biographical notes for the innumerable writers, musicians, and painters mentioned by Huysmans. This struck me as utterly useless, even if the notes were relegated to the back. Not only would they weigh the books down, but also you could never know whether you'd said too much—or not enough—about Lactance, Angela de Foligno, or Grünewald. Readers who wanted to know more could go find out for themselves, and that was that. As for the relationships between Huysmans and other writers of his time—Zola, Maupassant, Barbey d'Aurevilly, Gourmont, or Bloy—I thought these were best dealt with in the preface. Lacoue was quick to second this opinion.

Huysmans's use of obscure words and neologisms, on the other hand, did justify a certain amount of apparatus—I was imagining footnotes rather than endnotes, so as not to slow the reader down. He was enthusiastic in his agreement. "You've already done most of the work in your *Vertigos of Coining*!" he said heartily. I lifted my right hand in a gesture of deep reservation. On the contrary: in the book he was good enough to mention, I had barely touched on the question. No more than a quarter of Huysmans's linguistic corpus had been dealt with. He lifted his left hand in a gesture of deep appeasement: he certainly hadn't meant to understate the considerable work it would take to complete this edition. They hadn't set a deadline, I could rest easy on that score.

"Yes, you work for eternity . . ."

"It always sounds a little pretentious to say so, but yes—at least, that's the hope."

We shared a little moment of silence after this declaration, which was made with just the necessary drop of unction. It was going well, I'd say: we were coming together around shared values. This Pléiade was going to be a cinch.

"Robert Rediger was very sorry to see you leave the Sorbonne after the . . . the regime change," Lacoue began again, in a sadder voice. "I know because he's a friend of mine. A close friend." Now I detected a note of defiance. "Some teachers—senior teachers—stayed. Others, just as senior, left. Each one of those departures wounded him personally, including yours." This last he said almost gruffly, as if the duties of courtesy and friendship had been warring in his breast.

I had absolutely nothing to say to this, as he eventually realized after a minute or so of silence. "Well, I'm very happy that you've accepted my little project!" he exclaimed, rubbing his hands together, as if we were about to pull some kind of prank on the world of letters. "You know, I thought it was a shame that someone like you . . . someone at your level, I mean, should find himself out of work from one day to the next, with no publications—with nothing!" Aware that this might have sounded melodramatic, he stirred imperceptibly in his chair. I rose, too, with more alacrity.

•

Presumably in honor of the deal we'd just made, Lacoue didn't just walk me to the door but went with me down all three flights of stairs ("Careful, the steps are uneven!") and down the corridor ("It's a maze!" he laughed, but it wasn't really: there were two corridors that met at a right angle, and they led straight to the foyer), all the way to the front door of Éditions Gallimard, in the rue Gaston-Gallimard. The weather had grown brisk, and I suddenly realized that we hadn't discussed my fee. As if he'd read my mind, he brought a hand to my shoulder—without actually touching it—and said, "I'll be sending you a contract in the next couple of days. By the way," he added in the same breath, "there's going to be a little reception next Saturday for the reopening of the Sorbonne. I'll make sure you get an invitation. I know Robert would be very happy to see you there, if you're free." This time he gave me a real pat on the shoulder, then he shook my hand. It sounded off the cuff, but I had a feeling that, in reality, this invitation explained and justified all the rest.

The reception was at six, on the top floor of the Institute of the Arab World, which had been rented out for the occasion. I felt nervous as I showed my invitation: Who would be there? Some Saudis, definitely: the invitation guaranteed the presence of a Saudi prince whose name I recognized as that of the main donor behind the new Sorbonne. There would probably be some of my old colleagues, too, at least the ones who'd agreed to work under the new administration—but I didn't know anyone who had, except for Steve, and Steve was the last person I wanted to see.

I did recognize one former colleague, when I stepped inside the large, chandelier-lit hall. I didn't know him personally, though we'd spoken once or twice, but Bertrand de Gignac was world-famous in the field of medieval literature. He was regularly invited to lecture at Columbia and Yale, and he was the author of the standard reference work on the *Chanson de Roland*. As far as recruitment went, he was the one major success the new university president could claim. Beyond that, I didn't have much to talk to him about, the field of medieval literature being basically terra incognita to me, so I wisely accepted several mezes—they were excellent, the hot and the cold ones, too. So was the wine, a Lebanese red . . .

Still, I got the feeling that the reception wasn't a total success. Small groups of three to six people, Arab and French, made their way around the elegant hall, barely speaking. The Arabo-Andalusian background music, piercing and sinister, didn't help, but that wasn't the problem, and after walking around with the other guests for forty-five minutes, after a dozen mezes and four glasses of wine, I suddenly saw the problem: we were all men. No women had been invited, and to keep up a sociable atmosphere without any women around, and without falling back on soccer—which would have been inappropriate in what was, after all, an academic setting—turned out to be a serious challenge.

Just then I caught sight of Lacoue, standing in a thicker group that had retreated to a corner of the hall. Besides him there were maybe ten Arabs and two Frenchmen, all talking with great intensity, except for one middle-aged man with a hooked nose and a fat, scowling face. He was dressed simply, in a long white djellaba, but I could see he was the most important man in the group, probably the prince himself. The others were talking over one another, offering what seemed to be justifications, but he just stood there, and although he nodded his head every now and then, his face remained impassive. Clearly there was some kind of problem, but it had nothing to do with me, so I went back the way I came, accepting a cheese *samboussek* and fifth glass of wine.

An old, thin, very tall man with a long salt-and-pepper

beard went up to the prince, who stepped aside to speak to him in private. Having lost its center, the group instantly broke up. Wandering aimlessly through the hall with one of the other Frenchmen, Lacoue saw me and walked up with a small nod hello. He seemed out of his element, and he made his introductions so quietly that I didn't even catch the name of his companion, whose hair was slicked back, each strand carefully arranged. He wore a magnificent three-piece suit of midnight-blue fabric with nearly invisible white stripes. It had a light sheen and looked immensely soft. I thought it had to be silk and almost reached out to touch it, but I caught myself in time.

The prince, Lacoue explained, was furious because the minister of education hadn't come to the reception despite having formally promised to do so. Not only that—there wasn't a single representative from the ministry, not one, "not even the secretary of universities." He was beside himself.

"I already told you, there is no more secretary of universities," his companion growled. According to him, the situation was even worse than Lacoue thought: the minister had definitely meant to come, he'd confirmed just the day before, but Ben Abbes himself had intervened for the express purpose of humiliating the Saudis. This was in line with other recent measures, of much broader importance, such as relaunching the nuclear energy program and funding research into electric cars. The government was racing toward total independence from Saudi oil. Obviously, none of this had anything to do with the Islamic University of Paris–Sorbonne, but I supposed it was the university president who'd have to deal with the fallout. Just then Lacoue turned toward a middle-aged man, a new arrival, who was striding in our direction. "Here's Robert!" he cried, hugely relieved, as if he were greeting the Messiah.

Before he brought Rediger up to date, Lacoue introduced me, this time audibly. Rediger clasped my hand energetically, nearly crushing it between his powerful palms, all the while saying how happy he was to meet me and how long he'd looked forward to the pleasure. Physically, he was a fairly remarkable specimen, quite tall and solidly built. In fact, with his broad chest and his muscles, he looked more like a rugby tackle than a professor. His face was tan and deeply lined, and although his hair was completely white, it was very thick. He had a crew cut, and he was dressed, rather unexpectedly, in jeans and a black leather aviator jacket.

Lacoue quickly filled him in. Rediger nodded, and muttered that he'd had a feeling something like this might happen. Then he thought a moment. "I'll call Delhommais," he said. "Delhommais will know what to do." He took out a small, almost feminine cell phone—it looked tiny in his hand—and stepped a few meters away to make his call. Lacoue and his companion watched without daring to go near him, both rigid with suspense. They were starting to bore me, these two, with their little dramas. What's more, they struck me as complete idiots. Obviously these petrodollars required a certain amount of care and feeding, as it were, but in the end all they had to do was take some flunky and introduce him, not as the minister they'd seen on TV, but as his chief of staff. The joker in the three-piece suit would have made a perfect chief of staff (just to start with who was on hand) and the Saudis would have been none the wiser. Really, they were making everything more complicated than it needed to be. But that was their problem. I helped myself to another glass of wine and went out onto the terrace. The view of Notre-Dame truly was magnificent. It was warmer out than before, and the rain had stopped. The moonlight flickered over the ripples of the Seine.

•

I must have spent a long time in this reverie, and when I went back inside, the guests, still all men, of course, had thinned out. I didn't see Lacoue or the three-piece suit. At least the evening hadn't been a complete waste, I told myself, as I took a menu from the caterer. The mezes really had been good, plus they delivered—it would be a change from Indian. While I was waiting for my coat, Rediger walked up. "You're not leaving?" he asked, with a crestfallen spreading of the arms. I asked whether he'd managed to resolve the breach of protocol. "Yes, it's all sorted out. The minister won't come tonight, but he called the prince personally and invited him to breakfast tomorrow at the ministry. Schramek was right, I'm afraid: Ben Abbes is actively trying to humiliate them, now that he's reconnecting with his old friends the Qataris. We'll have plenty more trouble where that came from. But what can you do . . ." He waved the subject away, then he laid his hand on my shoulder. "I'm awfully sorry we didn't get a chance to talk. You should come over sometime for tea, so that we can have a real conversation . . ." And all at once he smiled. He had a lovely smile, very open, almost childlike, and extremely disarming in such a masculine man. I think he knew it, and knew how to use it. He gave me his card. "Next Wednesday, shall we say, five-ish? If you're free." I said I was.

In the metro I examined the business card that my new acquaintance had given me. It was elegant and tasteful, at least I thought so. Rediger provided his personal phone number, two office numbers, two fax numbers (one personal, one office), three e-mail addresses, ill defined, two cell numbers (one French, the other British), and a Skype handle. This was a man who let you know how to get in touch. Clearly, since my meeting with Lacoue, I'd made my way into the inner circle. It was almost unnerving.

He gave a street address, too: 5 rue des Arènes, and for now that was all I needed to know. I remembered the rue des Arènes. It was a charming little street off the Square des Arènes de Lutèce, in one of the most charming parts of Paris. There were butcher shops, cheese shops recommended by Petitrenaud and Pudlowski—as for Italian specialty shops, forget it. This was all reassuring in the extreme.

•

At the Place Monge metro station, I made the mistake of going out the Arènes de Lutèce exit. Geographically, I wasn't wrong—the exit led straight to the rue des Arènes—but I'd forgotten that there wasn't an escalator, and that the Place Monge metro station was fifty meters below street level. I was exhausted and out of breath by the time I emerged from that curious metro exit, a hollow carved out of the walls of the park, its thick columns, cubist typography, and generally neo-Babylonian appearance all completely out of place in Paris—as they would have been pretty much anywhere else in Europe.

When I reached 5 rue des Arènes, I realized that Rediger didn't just live in a charming street in the Fifth Arrondissement, he lived in his own *maison particulière* in a charming street in the Fifth Arrondissement, and that this *maison particulière* was *historic* to boot. Number 5 was none other than that fantastical neo-Gothic construction (flanked by a square turret like a castle keep) where Jean Paulhan lived from 1940 until his death in 1968. Personally I could never stand Jean Paulhan, I didn't like him as an éminence grise and I didn't like his books, but there was no denying that he'd been one of the most powerful figures in French publishing after the war. And he'd certainly lived in a very beautiful house. My admiration for the Saudis' funding only grew.

I rang the bell and was greeted by a butler whose cream-colored suit and Nehru collar were somewhat reminiscent of the former dictator Gadhafi. I told him my name, he bowed slightly: I was expected. He left me to wait in a little foyer, illuminated by stained-glass windows, while he went to tell Professor Rediger that I'd arrived.

I'd been waiting two or three minutes when a door opened to my left and in walked a teenage girl wearing low-waisted jeans and a Hello Kitty T-shirt, her long black hair loose over her shoulders. When she saw me, she shrieked, tried awkwardly to cover her face with her hands, and dashed back out of the room. At that very moment, Rediger appeared on the landing and came down the stairs to greet me. He had witnessed the incident, and shook my hand with a look of resignation.

"That's Aïcha, my new wife. She'll be very embarrassed that you saw her without her veil."

"I'm so sorry."

"No, don't apologize. It's her fault. She should have asked whether there was a guest before she came into the front hall. She doesn't know her way around the house yet, but she will."

"Yes, she looks very young."

"She just turned fifteen."

•

I followed Rediger up the stairs and into a large study with a ceiling that must have been almost five meters high. One of the walls was entirely covered with bookshelves. At a glance I noticed lots of old editions, mainly nineteenth century. Two solid metal ladders, mounted on rollers, provided access to the higher shelves. On the other side of the room, potted plants hung from a dark wooden trellis that ran the length of the wall. Ivy, ferns, and Virginia creeper cascaded from ceiling to floor, twining along the edges of various picture frames, some of which held hand-lettered verses from the Koran, others large, matted photos of galaxy clusters, supernovas, and spiral nebulas. In one corner a massive Directoire desk stood at an angle to the room. Rediger led me to the opposite corner, where two worn armchairs, upholstered in a red and green rep, were placed around a low, copper-topped table.

"I do have tea, if you like," he said, inviting me to sit. "Or perhaps a drink? I have whiskey, port—well, I have everything. And an excellent Meursault."

"The Meursault, then," I said, but I was a little bit confused. I had some idea that Islam prohibited drinking alcohol, at least that's what I'd heard. To be honest, it wasn't a religion I knew much about.

He left the room, presumably to see about the wine. My armchair faced a high, old, lead-mullioned window overlooking the Roman arena. The view was really something, I think it was the first time I'd had such a complete view of the terraces. And yet after a few minutes I found myself perusing the bookshelves. They were impressive, too.

The two bottom shelves were full of bound photocopies. These were dissertations from various European universities. As I browsed the titles, my eye was drawn to a philosophy dissertation, presented at the Catholic University of Louvain-la-Neuve, entitled "René Guénon: Reader of Nietzsche," by Robert Rediger. I was just pulling it from the shelf when Rediger came back into the room. I jumped, as if I'd been caught doing something wrong, and tried to slip it back in place. He walked over to me, smiling. "Don't worry, there are no secrets here. And besides, why shouldn't you be curious about the contents of a bookshelf? For a man like you, that's almost a professional duty."

Coming closer, he saw the title. "Ah, you've found my dissertation." He shook his head. "They gave me my doctorate, but it wasn't much of a thesis. Nothing like yours, anyway. My reading was, as they say, selective. In retrospect, I don't think Guénon was influenced by Nietzsche especially. His rejection of the modern world was just as vehement as Nietzsche's, but it had radically different sources. In any case, I'd write the thing very differently today. I have yours, too . . . ," he said, pulling another bound copy from the shelf. "As you know, we keep five copies in the university archives. So, considering how few researchers actually consult them in a given year, I thought I might as well keep one for myself."

I could barely hear what he was saying—I was on the verge of collapse. It was almost twenty years since I'd been in the presence of "Joris-Karl Huysmans: Out of the Tunnel." It was extraordinary how thick it was, almost embarrassing—it was, I suddenly remembered, 788 pages long. To be fair, it also contained seven years of my life.

Still holding my dissertation, he led us over to the armchairs. "It really is a remarkable piece of work . . . ," he insisted. "It reminded me very much of the young Nietzsche, the Nietzsche of *The Birth of Tragedy*."

"Please, you're exaggerating."

"I don't think I am. *The Birth of Tragedy* was, after all, a sort of dissertation. And in both you find the same incredible profligacy, the same profusion of ideas, all simply flung onto the page, without the slightest preparation so that, really, the text is almost impossible to read—the astonishing thing is that you managed to keep it up for almost eight hundred pages. By the time he wrote the *Untimely Meditations*, Nietzsche had calmed down. He realized that you can't overwhelm the reader with too many concepts at once, that you have to structure your argument and give him time to breathe. The same thing happened to you in *Vertigos of Coining*, which made it a more accessible book. The difference between you and Nietzsche is that Nietzsche kept going."

"I'm not Nietzsche."

"No, you're not. But you're you—and you're interesting. And if you'll forgive me for being blunt, I want you on my team. I might as well put my cards on the table, since you already know why you're here: I want to convince you to come back and teach at the Sorbonne. I want you to work for me."

At that moment the door opened, just in time to save me from having to answer. It was a plump woman, perhaps forty years old, with a kind face, carrying a tray of warm canapés arranged around an ice bucket. This held the promised bottle of Meursault.

"That's my first wife, Malika," he said once she'd left. "You seem to be meeting all my wives today. I married her when I was still living in Belgium . . . Yes, my family's Belgian. So am I, for that matter. I was never naturalized, though I've lived here for twenty years."

The canapés were delicious, spicy but not too; I tasted coriander. And the wine was sublime. "I don't think people talk enough about Meursault!" I said with gusto. "Meursault is a synthesis. It's like a lot of wines in one, don't you think?" I wanted to talk about anything besides my future as an academic, but I wasn't kidding myself. I knew he'd return to the subject at hand.

After a decent interval of silence, he returned to the subject at hand. "I'm so glad it worked out with the Pléiade edition. It's the obvious thing, the right thing—well, it's a good thing all around. When Lacoue mentioned it to me, what could I tell him? I said you'd be the natural choice, the right choice, and that you happened to be the best choice, too. Now, I'll be perfectly frank with you: apart from Gignac, I haven't managed to enlist any faculty who are truly eminent, who have real international reputations. It's hardly a disaster, the university just opened. But the fact is, I want something from you and I haven't got much to offer you in return. That is, I can offer you plenty of money, as you know, and money isn't nothing. But from an intellectual standpoint, a teaching position at the Sorbonne is much less prestigious than editing a Pléiade. I know that. What I can promise is that nothing would be allowed to interfere with your real work. That's a personal promise. No hard classes, just a couple of first- and second-year lectures. No dissertations to advise—I know what those are like, I've done enough of them myself. I'd fix everything with the department."

He stopped there. I got the distinct feeling that he'd used up his first round of arguments. He tasted the Meursault, I poured myself a second glass. It occurred to me that I had never felt so *desirable*. Glory had been a long time coming. Maybe my dissertation really had been as brilliant as he claimed, the truth was I remembered almost nothing about it; the intellectual leaps I made when I was young were a distant memory to me, and now I was surrounded by a kind of *aura*, when really my only goal in life was to do a little reading and get in bed at four in the afternoon with a carton of cigarettes and a bottle; and yet, at the same time, I had to admit, I was going to die if I kept that up—I was going to die fast, unhappy and alone. And did I really want to die fast, unhappy and alone? In the end, only kind of.

I finished my wine and poured myself a third glass. Through the bay window, I watched the sun setting over the arena. The silence became a little bit embarrassing. Well, if he wanted to *put his cards on the table*, two could play at that game.

"There's a condition, though . . . ," I said, cautiously. "And it isn't trivial . . ."

He gave a slow nod of the head.

"You think . . . You think I'm someone who could actually convert to Islam?"

He gazed at the floor, as if lost in intense personal reflections, then he looked me in the eye. "I do."

The smile he gave me was luminous, innocent. It was the second time he'd graced me with it, so it came as slightly less of a shock. But still, his smile was awfully effective. At least now it was his turn to talk. I swallowed two lukewarm canapés in quick succession. The sun vanished behind the terraced steps; night washed over the arena. It was amazing to think that fights between gladiators and wild beasts had actually taken place here, two thousand years before.

"You aren't Catholic, are you? That could be a problem."

No, in fact; I couldn't say that I was.

"And I don't guess you're really an atheist, either. True atheists are rare."

"You think? On the contrary, I'd have said that most people in the Western world are atheists."

"Only on the surface, it seems to me. The only true atheists I've ever met were people in *revolt*. It wasn't enough for them to coldly deny the existence of God—they had to refuse it, like Bakunin: 'Even if God existed, it would be necessary to abolish him.' They were atheists like Kirilov in *The Possessed*. They rejected God because they wanted to put man in his place. They were humanists, with lofty ideas about human liberty, human dignity. I don't suppose you recognize yourself in this description."

No, in fact, I didn't; even the word *humanism* made me want to vomit, but that might have been the canapés. I'd overdone it on the canapés. I took another glass of the Meursault to settle my stomach.

"The fact is, most people live their lives without worrying too much about these supposedly philosophical questions. They think about them only when they're facing some kind of tragedy—a serious illness, the death of a loved one. At least, that's how it is in the West; in the rest of the world people die and kill in the name of these very questions, they wage bloody wars over them, and they have since the dawn of time. These metaphysical questions are exactly what men fight over, not market shares or who gets to hunt where. Even in the West, atheism has no solid basis. When I talk to people about God, I always start by lending them a book on astronomy . . ."

"Your photos really are very beautiful."

"Yes, the beauty of the universe is striking, but the sheer size of it is what staggers the mind. You have hundreds of billions of galaxies, each made up of hundreds of billions of stars, some of them billions of light-years—hundreds of billions of billions of kilometers—apart. And if you pull back far enough, to a scale of a billion light-years, an order begins to emerge. The galaxy clusters are distributed according to a vast cosmic graph. If you go up to a hundred people in the street and lay out these scientific facts, how many will have the nerve to argue that the whole thing was created *by chance*? Besides, the universe is relatively young—fifteen billion years old at the most. It's like the famous monkey and the typewriter: How long would it take a chimpanzee, typing at random, to rewrite Shakespeare's plays? Well, how long would it take blind chance to reconstruct the universe? A lot more than fifteen billion years . . . And I'm not just speaking for the man in the street. The greatest scientists have thought so, too. In all of human history there may never have been a mind as brilliant as Isaac Newton's—just think what an amazing, unheard-of intellectual effort it took to discover a single law that accounted for the fall of earthly bodies *and* the movement of the planets! Well, Newton believed in God. He was such a firm believer that he spent the last years of his life writing an exegesis of the Bible—the one sacred text that was really available to him. Einstein wasn't an atheist, either. The exact nature of his belief is harder to define, but when he told Bohr, 'God does not play dice with the universe,' he didn't mean it as a joke. To him it was inconceivable that the universe should be ruled by chance. The argument of the 'watchmaker God,' which Voltaire considered irrefutable, is just as strong today as it was in the eighteenth century. If anything, it's become even more pertinent as science has drawn closer and closer connections between astrophysics and the motion of particles. At the end of the day, isn't there something ridiculous about some puny creature, living on an anonymous planet, in a remote spur of an ordinary galaxy, standing up on his hind legs and announcing, 'God does not exist'? But forgive me, I'm rambling . . ."

"No, don't apologize, I'm really interested," I said, sincerely. It's true that I was starting to feel a little bit fucked up. When I glanced over at the table, I saw that the bottle of Meursault was empty.

"You're right," I went on, "that I don't have any very solid grounds for my atheism. It would be presumptuous to claim that I did."

"*Presumptuous*—that's the word. At the end of the day, there's something incredibly proud and arrogant about atheist humanism. Even the Christian idea of incarnation is laughably pretentious. God turned Himself into a man . . . Why man and not an inhabitant of Sirius, or the Andromeda galaxy? Wouldn't that be more likely?"

"You believe in extraterrestrial life?" I interrupted. I was surprised.

"I don't know, I haven't given it much thought, but as a question of arithmetic, if you take all the myriad stars in the universe, each with its multiple planets, it would be shocking if life occurred only on earth. But that's not important. All I'm saying is that the universe obviously bears the hallmarks of intelligent design, that it's clearly the manifestation of some gigantic mind. Sooner or later, that simple idea is going to come back around. I've always known this, ever since I was young. All intellectual debate of the twentieth century can be summed up as a battle between communism—that is, 'hard' humanism—and liberal democracy, the soft version. But what a reductive debate. Since I was fifteen, I've known that what they now call the return of religion was unavoidable. My family was Catholic—or rather, they were lapsed; really it was my grandparents who were Catholic—so naturally I started off turning toward the Church. Then, in my first year at university, I joined the nativist movement."

My surprise must have shown, because he stopped and looked at me, a smile playing on his lips. Just then there was a knock at the door and Malika reappeared carrying a new tray with a *cafetière*, two cups, and a plate of pistachio baklava and *briouats*. She also brought in a bottle of *boukha*, with two small glasses.

•

Rediger poured us coffee. It was bitter and very strong, and it did me good. My head was instantly clear.

"I've never hidden my youthful activities," he went on. "And my new Muslim friends never held them against me. To them it seemed natural that, when I started looking for a way out of atheist humanism, I should have gone back to my roots. Besides, we weren't racists or fascists—though, to be completely honest, some of us were pretty close. But not me. Fascism always struck me as a ghastly, nightmarish, false attempt to breathe life into dead nations. Without Christianity, the European nations had become bodies without souls—zombies. The question was, could Christianity be revived? I thought so. I thought so for several years—with growing doubts. As time went on, I subscribed more and more to Toynbee's idea that civilizations die not by murder but by suicide. And then one day everything changed for me. It was March thirtieth, 2013, I'll never forget—Easter weekend. At the time I was living in Brussels, and every once in a while I'd go have a drink at the bar of the Métropole. I'd always loved Art Nouveau. There are magnificent examples in Prague and Vienna, and there are interesting buildings in Paris and London, too, but for me—right or wrong—the high point of Art Nouveau decor was the Hotel Métropole de Bruxelles, in particular the bar. The morning of March thirtieth, I happened to walk by and saw a sign that said the bar of the Métropole was closing for good, that very night. I was stunned. I went in and spoke to the waiters. They confirmed it; they didn't know the exact reasons. To think that, until then, one could order sandwiches and beer, Viennese chocolates, and cakes with cream in that absolute masterpiece of decorative art, that one could live one's daily life surrounded by beauty, and that the whole thing was about to disappear, in one stroke, in one of the capitals of Europe! . . . Yes, that was the moment I understood: Europe had already committed suicide. As a reader of Huysmans, you must sometimes get tired of his relentless pessimism, his endless railing against the mediocrity of his times. I know I do. In fact, he was living at a time when the European nations were at their apogee, when they commanded vast colonial empires, and dominated the world! . . . It was an extraordinary moment, technologically—railroads, electric lighting, the telephone, the phonograph, Eiffel's steel constructions—and also artistically, but here there are too many names to mention, whether you look at literature, painting, or music . . ."

He was right, of course. In the "art of living" alone, there had been a serious falling-off. As Rediger offered me a baklava, which I accepted, I thought of a book I had read some years before, on the history of brothels. The frontispiece featured a brochure from a Parisian brothel of the Belle Époque. It came as a profound shock when I realized that some of the sexual specialties offered by "Mademoiselle Hortense" were completely unknown to me. I had no idea what a "voyage through the yellow land" or a "Russian imperial soap" could possibly mean. Certain sexual practices had vanished from human memory, in one century—not unlike certain forms of skilled labor, such as cobbling or bell-ringing. How could anyone argue that Europe wasn't in decline?

"That Europe, which was the summit of human civilization, committed suicide in a matter of decades." Rediger's voice was sad. He'd left all the overhead lights off; the only illumination came from the lamp on his desk. "Throughout Europe there were anarchist and nihilist movements, calls for violence, the denial of moral law. And then a few years later it all came to an end with the unjustifiable madness of the First World War. Freud was not wrong, and neither was Thomas Mann: if France and Germany, the two most advanced, civilized nations in the world, could unleash this senseless slaughter, then Europe was dead. I spent that last night at the Métropole, until it closed. I walked all the way home, halfway across the city, past the EU compound, that gloomy fortress in the slums. The next day I went to see an imam in Zaventem. And the day after that—Easter Monday— in front of a handful of witnesses, I spoke the ritual words and converted to Islam."

•

I wasn't sure I agreed about the crucial importance of the First World War; it had been an inexcusable slaughter, no question, but the War of 1870 had been fairly absurd, too, at least according to Huysmans's description, and had already seriously eroded patriotic feeling of all kinds. Nations were a murderous absurdity, and after 1870 anyone paying attention had probably figured this out. That's when nihilism, anarchism, and all that crap started. As for older civilizations, I wasn't really up to speed. Night had fallen on the square; the last tourists had already left; here and there a lone street-light shed its feeble beams on the steps of the arena. No doubt the Romans had felt that theirs was an eternal civilization, right up to the moment their empire fell apart. Were they suicides, too? Rome had been a brutal civilization and very competent militarily—a cruel civilization, too, where men fought to the death, or fought animals to the death, just to keep the mob entertained. Did the Romans wish they could disappear? Was that their secret flaw? Rediger had certainly read Gibbon, and other writers like that who were just names to me. I didn't really feel able to keep up my end of the conversation.

"I really do talk too much," he said, with a dismissive wave. He poured me a glass of *boukha* and held out the pastries again. They were excellent, and the contrast with the bitterness of the fig brandy was delicious. "It's late. I should really go," I said uncertainly. The truth was I didn't really want to leave.

"Wait!" He got up and went over to his desk. Behind it, the shelves were full of dictionaries and reference books. He came back with a small, illustrated paperback, inscribed to me, entitled *Ten Questions on Islam.*

"Here I am, proselytizing at you for three hours, when I've already written a book on the subject. I guess it's become second nature . . . But maybe you've heard of it?"

"Yes, it sold very well, didn't it?"

"Three million copies," he apologized. "I seem to have developed an unexpected knack for the middlebrow. It's awfully schematic, of course . . . ," he apologized again. "But at least it's a quick read."

It was 128 pages long, with lots of pictures, mainly Islamic art. He was right, it wouldn't take me too long. I put it in my backpack.

He poured us two more glasses of *boukha.* Outside, the moon had risen high over the terraces of the arena, and now it outshone the streetlights. I noticed that the verses from the Koran and the photographs of galaxies, hung amid the wall of vegetation, were lit by small individual lamps.

•

"Your house is very beautiful . . ."

"It took me years to get here. Believe me, it wasn't easy."

He shifted in his chair, and now, for the first time since I'd arrived, I had the feeling that he was actually unbending, he was about to speak from the heart: "Obviously, I have no interest in Paulhan—who could be interested in Paulhan? But it *is* a constant source of happiness to think that I live in the house where Dominique Aury wrote *Story of O*—or, at least, in the house of the lover she wrote it for. It's a fascinating book, don't you think?"

I completely agreed. In principle, *Story of O* contained everything I didn't like in a novel: other people's fantasies disgusted me, and the whole thing was so ostentatiously kitschy—the apartment on the Île Saint-Louis, the *hôtel particulier* in the Faubourg Saint-Germain, *Sir Stephen*, all that stuff was for shit. Still, the book had a passion, a vitality that swept everything before it.

"It's submission," Rediger murmured. "The shocking and simple idea, which had never been so forcefully expressed, that the summit of human happiness resides in the most absolute submission. I hesitate to discuss the idea with my fellow Muslims, who might consider it sacrilegious, but for me there's a connection between woman's submission to man, as it's described in *Story of O*, and the Islamic idea of man's submission to God. You see," he went on, "Islam accepts the world, and accepts it whole. It accepts the world *as such*, Nietzsche might say. For Buddhism, the world is *dukkha*—unsatisfactoriness, suffering. Christianity has serious reservations of its own. Isn't Satan called 'the prince of the world'? For Islam, though, the divine creation is perfect, it's an absolute masterpiece. What is the Koran, really, but one long mystical poem of praise? Of praise for the Creator, and of submission to his laws. In general, I don't think it's a good idea to learn about Islam by reading the Koran, unless of course you take the trouble to learn Arabic and read the original text. What I tell people to do instead is listen to the suras read aloud, and repeat them, so you can feel their breath and their force. In any case, Islam is the only religion where it's forbidden to use any translations in the liturgy, because the Koran is made up entirely of rhythms, rhymes, refrains, assonance. It starts with the idea, the basic idea of all poetry, that sound and sense can be made one, and so can speak the world."

Once again, he looked apologetic. I think he was half pretending to be embarrassed by his own proselytizing, but he must also have been aware of having used this same speech with so many other academics. I bet the part about not translating the Koran was what hooked Gignac: those medievalists always hate to see the object of their devotion translated into modern French. But still, even if his arguments were well rehearsed, that didn't take away from their strength. And look at how he lived: a forty-year-old wife to do the cooking, a fifteen-year-old wife for whatever else . . . No doubt he had one or two wives in between, but I couldn't think how to ask. This time I got up to leave for real. I thanked him for a fascinating afternoon, which had turned into a fascinating evening. He told me it had been a great pleasure for him, too—in short, we had a sort of attack of politeness on his doorstep; but we both meant every word we said.

Back at home, after tossing and turning for an hour, I realized I wasn't going to fall asleep. The only thing I had in the house to drink was a bottle of rum. It wouldn't mix well with the *boukha*, but I needed it. For the first time in my life I'd started thinking about God, seriously imagining that there could be a kind of Creator of the universe observing everything I did, and my first reaction was uncomplicated, pure and simple fear. Gradually I calmed down, with the help of the alcohol, by telling myself that I was a relatively insignificant individual, that the Creator certainly had better things to do, etc., but the terrifying idea persisted that he might suddenly become aware of my existence, that he would *lay his hand* on me, and that I'd be stricken with cancer of the jaw, for example, like Huysmans. It was a cancer that smokers often got, Freud had it, too. Yes, cancer of the jaw seemed plausible. What would I do once they removed my jaw? How could I go out into the street, go to the supermarket, buy groceries—how could I stand all those looks of pity and disgust? And if I couldn't buy groceries, who'd buy them for me? The night ahead was long, and I felt dramatically alone. Would I at least have the base-level courage to kill myself? I didn't even know.

I woke up around six in the morning, seriously hungover. While the coffee was brewing, I went looking for *Ten Questions on Islam*, but after fifteen minutes I had to face the obvious: my backpack wasn't there. I'd left it at Rediger's.

After two aspirin, I felt strong enough to consult a dictionary of theater slang, published in 1907, in which I managed to find two rare words used by Huysmans that might well have been mistaken for neologisms. This was the fun part of my work, fun and relatively easy. The hard part would be the preface. I knew that's what everyone was waiting for. Sooner or later, I'd have to go back and reread my own dissertation. The thought of those eight hundred pages was terrifying, almost crushing; as far as I remembered, I'd interpreted Huysmans's work in the light of his future conversion. The author himself encouraged this, and no doubt I let myself be manipulated by him. His own preface to *À rebours*, written twenty years later, was symptomatic. Did *À rebours* really lead, inevitably, to a return to the Church? In the end Huysmans did return to the Church, and clearly he meant it. *Les foules de Lourdes*, his last book, was authentically the work of a Christian, in which the misanthropic aesthete and loner overcomes his aversion to religious trinkets and finally allows himself to be carried away by the simple faith of the pilgrims at Lourdes. On the other hand, practically speaking, this return didn't require much in the way of personal sacrifice: as a lay brother at Ligugé, Huysmans was allowed to live outside the monastery. He had his own housekeeper, who cooked him the bourgeois meals that played such a prominent role in his life. He had his library and his packets of Dutch tobacco. He did all the offices, and no doubt he enjoyed them: his aesthetic, almost carnal delight in the Catholic liturgy comes through on every page of his later books. As for the metaphysical questions that Rediger had raised the night before, Huysmans never mentions them. The infinite spaces that terrified Pascal, that inspired in Newton and Kant such awe and respect, Huysmans seems never to have noticed. He was a convert, certainly, but not along the lines of Péguy or Claudel. My own dissertation, I now realized, would not be much help to me; and neither would Huysmans's own protestations of faith.

•

Around ten that morning, I decided that it was a decent hour to ring the bell at 5 rue des Arènes. The same butler greeted me with a smile, still wearing his white Nehru suit. Rediger was out, he told me, and yes, I had indeed left something behind. Thirty seconds later, he brought me my Adidas bag. Rediger must have put it aside early that morning. He was polite, efficient, and discreet. In a sense, I found Rediger even more impressive than his wives. He must have cut through red tape like a flash, with a snap of his fingers.

As I walked back along the rue de Quatrefages, I found myself—entirely by accident—in front of the Paris Mosque. My thoughts turned not to the ultimate Creator of the universe but, crassly enough, to Steve: clearly, they'd lowered their standards. I was no Gignac, but still, if I decided to go back to work, I could be sure they'd welcome me with open arms.

By contrast, my decision to keep going down the rue Daubenton, toward the Sorbonne–Paris III, was entirely conscious. I wasn't planning to go in, I just wanted to walk past the gates, but I felt a pang of joy when I recognized the Senegalese guard. He was beaming, too. "Happy to see you, monsieur! It's good to have you back!" I didn't have the heart to disabuse him, and so when he waved me through, I ventured inside the courtyard. I had spent fifteen years of my life at this school. I was glad to recognize one person, at least. I wondered if he'd had to convert, too, to get his job back. But maybe he already was a Muslim, some Senegalese are—at least I think so.

I spent fifteen minutes strolling under the arcades with their metal beams, slightly surprised by my own nostalgia and aware, at the same time, that the place really was extremely ugly. Those hideous buildings had been constructed during the worst period of modernism, but nostalgia has nothing to do with aesthetics, it's not even connected to happy memories. We feel nostalgia for a place simply because we've lived there; whether we lived well or badly scarcely matters. The past is always beautiful. So, for that matter, is the future. Only the present hurts, and we carry it around like an abscess of suffering, our companion between two infinities of happiness and peace.

Gradually, after I'd walked around enough under the metal beams, my nostalgia faded, and I almost stopped thinking altogether. I did think of Myriam, briefly but very painfully, as I went past the snack bar where we first met.

Nowadays, of course, all the female students wore veils, mainly white veils, and as they strolled in groups of two or three under the arcades, the place had the look of a convent— at any rate, the overall impression was undeniably studious. I wondered how it must be to see them in the older setting of the Sorbonne–Paris IV, whether it felt like going back to the time of Abélard and Héloïse.

Ten Questions on Islam was indeed a simple book, and very efficiently structured. The first chapter, answering the question "What do we believe?" didn't have much to teach me. It was basically what Rediger had said the afternoon before about the vastness and harmony of the universe, the perfection of its design, etc. Then came a brief outline of the prophets, culminating in Muhammad.

Like most men, probably, I skipped the chapters on religious duties, the pillars of wisdom, and child-rearing, and went straight to chapter 7: "Why Polygamy?" The argument was original, I have to say: to realize his sublime plan in the inanimate world, the Creator of the universe used the laws of geometry (a non-Euclidean geometry, to be sure, a non-commutative geometry, but still a geometry). When it came to living beings, however, the Creator expressed himself through natural selection, which allowed animate creatures to achieve their maximum beauty, vitality, and power. And for all animal species, including man, the law was the same:

only certain individuals would be chosen to pass on their seed, to conceive the next generation, on which an infinite number of generations depended. In the case of mammals, if you compared the female, with her long gestation period, to the male, with his essentially limitless capacity to reproduce, it was clear that the pressures of selection would fall principally on the males. If some males enjoyed access to several females, others would necessarily have none. So this inequality between males should be considered not a negative side effect of polygamy but rather its goal. It was how the species achieved its destiny.

These curious considerations led directly to chapter 8, "Ecology and Islam." It was a less controversial chapter. As Rediger saw it, halal food was like a kind of improved organic diet. As for chapters 9 and 10, which had to do with economics and political institutions, they seemed to have been written specifically in support of Mohammed Ben Abbes.

In this work, which was meant for a very broad readership, and which found one, Rediger made lots of concessions to the humanist reader. He spent a long time comparing Islam with the brutal herding civilizations that preceded it. He argued that Islam had not invented polygamy but rather had helped regulate it, that Islam was not the origin of stoning or female circumcision, that the Prophet Muhammad had urged masters to free their slaves, and that by establishing the principle that all men were equal before their Creator, he had put an end to racial discrimination in every land he conquered.

I knew all those arguments, I'd heard them a thousand

times, though that didn't mean they were wrong. But what had struck me during our meeting—and struck me even more now as I read his book—was that sense of hearing a *well-rehearsed speech*, which inevitably made Rediger sound like a politician. Politics hadn't come up that afternoon on the rue des Arènes; but a week later I wasn't surprised to see that, thanks to some minor ministerial reshuffling, Rediger had been named secretary of universities—a post they'd revived just for him.

In the meantime, I'd had occasion to discover that he was decidedly less cautious in his articles for more specialized magazines, such as the *Review of Palestinian Studies* or *Oumma*. The lack of curiosity displayed by journalists really was a blessing for intellectuals: all of these articles were easily accessible on the Web, and in certain cases, it seemed to me, would have been worth the trouble of digging up. But I may have been wrong; over the course of the twentieth century, plenty of intellectuals had supported Stalin, Mao, or Pol Pot and had never been taken to task. For the French, an intellectual didn't have to be *responsible*. That wasn't his job.

In an article for *Oumma*, Rediger raised the question whether Islam had been chosen for world domination. In the end he answered yes. He hardly bothered with Western societies, since to him they seemed so obviously doomed (liberal individualism triumphed as long as it undermined intermediate structures such as nations, corporations, castes, but when it attacked that ultimate social structure, the family, and thus the birthrate, it signed its own death warrant; Muslim dominance was a foregone conclusion). He had more to say about India and China: if India and China had preserved their traditional civilizations, he wrote, they might have remained strangers to monotheism and eluded the grasp of Islam. But from the moment they let themselves be contaminated by Western values, they, too, were doomed: he detailed the process and offered a preliminary time-table. The article, cogent and well sourced, clearly betrayed the influence of Guénon, who drew the same basic distinction between traditional societies, considered as a whole, and modern civilization.

In another article, Rediger made a case for highly un-equal wealth distribution. Although an authentic Muslim society would have to abolish actual destitution (alms-giving was one of the Five Pillars of Wisdom), it should also main-tain a wide gap between the masses, who would live in self-respecting poverty, and a tiny minority of individuals so fantastically rich that they could throw away vast, insane sums, thus assuring the survival of luxury and the arts. This aristocratic position came directly from Nietzsche; deep down, Rediger had remained remarkably faithful to the thinkers of his youth.

He was similarly Nietzschean in his sarcastic, withering hostility toward Christianity, which according to him was based on the decadent, antisocial personality of Jesus. The founder of Christianity enjoyed the company of women, he wrote, *and it showed*. He quoted Nietzsche's *Anti-Christ*: " 'If Islam despises Christianity, it has a thousandfold right to do so; Islam at least assumes that it is dealing with *men . . .*' " The idea of Christ's divinity, Rediger went on, led directly to humanism and the "rights of man." This, too, Nietzsche had already said, and in harsher terms, and for the same reasons he would certainly have signed on to the idea that Islam had a mission to rid the world of the pernicious doctrine of the incarnation.

As I got older, I also found myself agreeing more with Nietzsche, as is no doubt inevitable once your plumbing starts to fail. And I found myself more interested in Elohim, the sublime organizer of the constellations, than in his insipid offspring. Jesus had loved men too much, that was the problem; to let himself be crucified for their sake showed, at the very least, *a lack of taste*, as the old faggot would have put it. And the rest of his actions weren't any more discerning, like when he absolved the adulterous woman, for example, with arguments such as "let him who is without sin," etc. All you'd have had to do was get hold of a seven-year-old child—he'd have cast the first stone, the little fucker.

•

Rediger was a good writer. He was clear and concise, and occasionally humorous, as for example when he derided a colleague—no doubt a rival Muslim intellectual—who had coined the phrase "imams 2.0" to describe imams who made it their mission to reconvert French youth from Muslim immigrant backgrounds. It was time, Rediger countered, to launch imams 3.0: the ones who'd convert the natives. Rediger was never funny for long; he always followed up with an earnest argument. He reserved his bitterest scorn for his Islamo-leftist colleagues: Islamo-leftism, he wrote, was a desperate attempt by moldering, putrefying, brain-dead Marxists to hoist themselves out of the dustbin of history by latching onto the coattails of Islam. Conceptually, he wrote, they'd stolen everything from the so-called Nietzscheans of the left. Rediger was obsessed with Nietzsche, but I didn't have much patience for his Nietzschean mode—no doubt I'd read too much Nietzsche myself. I knew and understood Nietzsche too well to find him charming. Bizarrely enough, I found myself more drawn to Rediger's Guénonian side. René Guénon is boring, if you try to read him straight through, but Rediger offered an accessible version—Guénon lite. I especially liked an article entitled "Geometry of the Link," in the *Review of Traditional Studies*. There Rediger reconsidered the failure of communism, which was, after all, an early attempt to combat liberal individualism. He argued that Stalin was wrong and Trotsky was right: communism could triumph only if it was global, and the same held true for Islam: either it would become universal, or it would cease to exist. But most of the article was a strange meditation, rather kitschily Spinozan—there were scholia, numbered propositions, etc.—on the theory of graphs. Only religion, the article tried to show, could create a total relationship between individuals. Think of an X-Y graph, Rediger wrote, with individuals (points) linked according to their personal relationships: it is impossible to construct a graph in which each individual is linked to every other. The only solution is to create a higher plane, containing one point called God, to which all of the individuals can be linked—and linked to one another, through this intermediary.

All that stuff made for very good reading; even though geometrically his proof didn't make any sense, it took my mind off my plumbing. In general my intellectual life was at a standstill: I was making progress on the footnotes, but I still couldn't get started on the preface. Oddly enough, it was an Internet search on Huysmans that led me to one of Rediger's most remarkable articles, this one in the *European Review*. He mentioned Huysmans only in passing, as the author who best exemplified the dead end of Naturalism and materialism; but the whole article was one long appeal to his old comrades, the traditional nativists. It was a passionate plea. He called it tragic that their irrational hostility to Islam should blind them to the obvious: on every question that really mattered, the nativists and the Muslims were in perfect agreement. When it came to rejecting atheism and humanism, or the necessary submission of women, or the return of patriarchy, they were fighting exactly the same fight. And today this fight, to establish a new organic phase of civilization, could no longer be waged in the name of Christianity. Islam, its sister faith, was newer, simpler, and more true (why had Guénon, for example, converted to Islam? he was above all a man of science, and he had chosen Islam on scientific grounds, both for its conceptual economy and to avoid certain marginal, irrational doctrines such as the real presence of Christ in the eucharist), which is why Islam had taken up the torch. Thanks to the simpering seductions and the lewd enticements of the progressives, the Church had lost its ability to oppose moral decadence, to renounce homosexual marriage, abortion rights, and women in the workplace. The facts were plain: Europe had reached a point of such putrid decomposition that it could no longer save itself, any more than fifth-century Rome could have done. This wave of new immigrants, with their traditional culture—of natural hierarchies, the submission of women, and respect for elders—offered a historic opportunity for the moral and familial rearmament of Europe. These immigrants held out the hope of a new golden age for the old continent. Some were Christian; but there was no denying that the vast majority were Muslim.

He, Rediger, was the first to admit the greatness of medieval Christendom, whose artistic achievements would live forever in human memory; but little by little it had given way, it had been forced to compromise with rationalism, it had renounced its temporal powers, and so had sealed its own doom—and why? In the end, it was a mystery; God had ordained it so.

Not long afterward I received Rigaud's *Dictionnaire d'argot moderne* (Ollendorff, 1881), which I'd ordered weeks before and which helped me clear up certain questions that had been nagging at me. As I had suspected, *claquedent* was not a coinage original to Huysmans; it was slang for a whore-house, just as a *clapier* denoted any place of prostitution. Nearly all of Huysmans's sexual relations had taken place with prostitutes, and his letters to Arij Prins were exhaustive on the subject of European brothels. As I perused these letters, I suddenly got the feeling that I had to go to Brussels. I wasn't sure where this feeling came from. Of course, Huysmans had been published in Brussels, but then, nearly every important author of the second half of the nineteenth century had, at one time or another, been forced to engage the services of a Belgian publisher in order to get around the censors, the same way Huysmans did, and when I was writing my dissertation I hadn't seen any compelling reason to make the trip. I had gone a few years later, but that was mainly because of Baudelaire. What struck me most about Brussels was the filth and sadness of the city, and the ethnic hatred, which was even more palpable than in Paris or London. In Brussels, more than in any other European capital, you felt on the edge of civil war.

Now the Muslim Party of Belgium had just won the national elections. This was generally considered big news for the balance of European politics. Of course, the Muslim parties already occupied government seats in Britain, Holland, and Germany, but Belgium was the second country, after France, where the Muslims had won an outright majority. The stinging defeat of the European right had a simple explanation, in Belgium's case: although the Flemish and Walloon nationalist parties enjoyed overwhelming support in their native regions, they'd never managed to work together, or even to engage in any real dialogue, whereas the Flemish and Walloon Muslim parties, with their shared religion, had no trouble forming a coalition.

Ben Abbes had immediately issued a warm statement hailing the victory of the Muslim Party of Belgium. As it happens, the secretary general, Raymond Stouvenens, had a personal history not unlike Rediger's: before he converted to Islam, he'd been a high-ranking member of a nativist organization, though he'd kept his distance from its openly neofascist wing.

•

The café car on the Thalys to Brussels had two menus, one traditional and one halal. That was the first transformation I noticed—and the only one. The streets were just as filthy, and the Hotel Métropole, even if its bar was closed, had preserved much of its old splendor. When the train got in, around nine thirty, it was even colder than in Paris. The sidewalks were covered in blackish snow. I was sitting in a restaurant in the rue de la Montagne-aux-Herbes-Potagères, trying to decide between a chicken *waterzooi* and an *anguille au vert*, when all at once I was gripped by the certainty that I understood Huysmans completely, better than he had understood himself, and that I was finally able to write my preface. I had to get back to the hotel and make some notes, and left the restaurant without ordering. (The room service menu offered chicken *waterzooi*, which settled that.) It had been a mistake to give too much importance to Huysmans's glib talk about "debauches" and "dissipation." That was just a Naturalist tic, a contemporary cliché, part of the need to scandalize, to shock the bourgeoisie. In the end, it was a career move; and the opposition he set up between carnal appetite and the rigors of monastic life was equally beside the point. Chastity wasn't a problem and never had been, not for Huysmans or anyone else. My brief stay at Ligugé had only confirmed this for me. Subject man to erotic stimuli, even in their most standardized form—something as simple as low necklines and short skirts (or in the apt Spanish phrase, *tetas y culo*)—and he will feel sexual desire. Remove said stimuli and the desire will go away, and in a matter of months or even weeks he won't even remember his sexuality. In reality this had never posed the least difficulty for monks, and in my own case, as the new Islamic regime pushed women's clothing in the direction of decency, I had felt my own sexual impulses gradually diminish. I sometimes went whole days without thinking of sex. With women it might be slightly different, since for women erotic stimuli were more diffuse and thus harder to overcome, but I really didn't have time to go into that right now, I was taking notes in a frenzy (after I finished my *waterzooi* I ordered a cheese plate), not only had sex mattered less to Huysmans than he thought, but in the end the same was true of death. Existential anguish simply wasn't his thing, what had really struck him about Grünewald's famous Crucifixion wasn't Christ's agony but rather his physical suffering, and in this Huysmans was just like everybody else. People don't really care all that much about their own death. What they really worry about, their one real fixation, is how to avoid physical suffering as much as possible. Even in the realm of art criticism, Huysmans got it all wrong. He had passionately sided with the Impressionists when they ran up against the academic precepts of their time, he had written admiring pages on painters like Gustave Moreau and Odilon Redon; but in his own novels, he identified less with Impressionism or Symbolism than with the much older pictorial tradition of the Dutch masters. In the end, the dream visions of *En rade*, which actually did recall the strangeness of certain Symbolist paintings, were a failure. At least, they leave a much less vivid impression than his warm, precisely detailed descriptions of meals with the Carhaixes in *Là-bas*. That's when I realized I'd left my copy of *Là-bas* in Paris. I had to go back. According to the website, the first Thalys left at five. By seven a.m. I was home and I looked up the passages where he described the cooking of "Maman Carhaix." Huysmans's true subject had been bourgeois happiness, a happiness painfully out of reach for a bachelor, and not the happiness of the haute bourgeoisie (the cooking celebrated in *Là-bas* was instead what you might call good home cooking), much less that of the aristocracy. Huysmans had nothing but contempt for the "titled fools" he ridiculed in *L'oblat*. His idea of happiness was to have his artist friends over for a pot-au-feu with horseradish sauce, accompanied by an "honest" wine and followed by plum brandy and tobacco, with everyone sitting by the stove while the winter winds battered the towers of Saint-Sulpice. These simple pleasures had been denied him, and only someone as crude and insensitive as Bloy could have been surprised to see him weep over the death, in 1895, of Anna Meunier, his one lasting female acquaintance, the only woman he had ever been able to live with, briefly, until her nervous malady, incurable at the time, sent her into the Saint-Anne asylum.

Later in the day I went out and bought five packs of cigarettes, then I found the menu from that Lebanese caterer, and two weeks later my preface was done. A low-pressure system had entered France from the Azores, there was something balmy and springlike in the air, a kind of suspicious sweetness. Only a year ago, under the same meteorological conditions, you'd have seen the arrival of the first short skirts. I walked down the avenue de Choisy, then the avenue des Gobelins, and turned onto the rue Monge. In a café near the Institute of the Arab World, I reread the forty pages I had written. Some of the punctuation needed correcting, a few of the references still had to be filled in, but even so, there was no doubt about it: it was the best thing I'd ever written, the best thing ever written on Huysmans, period.

I made my way home slowly on foot, like a little old man, more aware with every step that this time my intellectual life really was over; and that so was my long, very long relationship with Joris-Karl Huysmans.

Naturally, I didn't say anything to Bastien Lacoue. I knew it would be at least a year, maybe two, before he got worried and gave me a deadline. I had all the time in the world to refine my footnotes. My immediate future promised to be, as they say in English, *supercool.*

Or maybe just cool, I hedged, as I opened my mailbox for the first time since I'd gotten back from Brussels; there were still bureaucratic headaches to deal with, and bureaucracy "never sleeps."

I didn't have the courage to open any of the envelopes just yet. I had spent the past two weeks in what you might call *the realms of the ideal.* In my own small way, I had *created.* To go back to my status as an ordinary cog in the bureaucratic machine felt slightly jarring. I did see one not-quite-bureaucratic envelope from the Islamic University of Paris IV–Sorbonne. Aha, I thought to myself.

My "aha" took on new dimensions as I read the contents of the letter: I was invited, the very next day, to the ceremony welcoming Jean-François Loiseleur into his new position of university professor. There would be an official reception in the Richelieu amphitheater, with a speech, then a cocktail party in an adjacent suite set aside for the purpose.

I remembered Loiseleur very well. He was the one who first introduced me to the *Journal of Nineteenth-Century Studies*, years ago. He had joined the faculty after publishing a groundbreaking dissertation on the poems of Leconte de Lisle. Because he was considered one of the two leaders of the Parnassians, along with Heredia, Leconte de Lisle tended to be dismissed as "workmanlike and uninspired," in the anthologists' phrase. As an old man, however, in the wake of some kind of mystico-cosmological crisis, Leconte de Lisle had written some strange poems that were unlike anything he or anyone else had ever written. In fact, no one had ever known what to make of them, beyond pointing out that they had all been *completely bonkers*. Loiseleur could take credit for having unearthed these poems, and for having managed to say something about them, although he wasn't able to place them in any real literary tradition—according to him, it made more sense to situate them in relation to certain intellectual phenomena known to the aging Parnassian, such as theosophy or spiritualism. In this way Loiseleur acquired, in a field where he had no rivals, a certain notoriety—not the international status of a Gignac, to be sure, but he was regularly invited to give lectures at Oxford and St. Andrews.

In person, Loiseleur was a remarkably good match for his subject. I have never met anyone so reminiscent of the comic-strip hero Cosinus. With his long, gray, dirty hair, his

Coke-bottle glasses, and his mismatched suits, generally in a state that approached the unhygienic, he inspired a kind of pitying respect. It's not that he was trying to *play a character*: that's just the way he was, he couldn't help it. For all that, he was the kindest, sweetest man in the world, and completely without vanity. The act of teaching—implying, as it did, a certain amount of contact with people of different backgrounds—had always terrified him. How had Rediger managed to hire him back? I would go to the cocktail party, at least; I wanted to know.

•

With their modest historical cachet, and genuinely prestigious address, the reception rooms at the Sorbonne were never used for academic functions in my day, although they were often rented out at indecent rates for runway shows and other *red carpet* events; it may not have been very honorable, but it paid the bills. The new Saudi proprietors had put an end to all that. Thanks to them, the place had regained a certain scholarly dignity. As I entered the first room, I was happy to spot the logo of the Lebanese caterers who'd kept me company the entire time I was working on my preface. By now I knew the menu by heart, and I ordered with authority. The guests were the usual mix of French academics and Arab dignitaries, but this time there were plenty of Frenchmen. It looked as if the entire faculty had come. That was understandable enough. Many people still considered it slightly shameful to bow down to the new Saudi regime, as if it were an act of *collaboration*, so to speak; by gathering together, the teachers showed strength in numbers and gave one another courage. And they took special satisfaction in welcoming a new colleague into their midst.

No sooner had I been served my mezes than I found myself face-to-face with Loiseleur. He had changed. Although not exactly presentable, his exterior was much improved. His hair, still long and dirty, almost looked as if someone had combed it; his jacket and trousers were the same color, pretty much, and unembellished by any grease stain or cigarette burn. One couldn't help detecting a woman's hand at work—at least that was my guess.

"Um, yes . . . ," he answered, without my having asked him anything. "I *took the plunge.* Funny, I'd never thought of doing it before, but it's actually very pleasant. I'm very glad to see you, by the way. How are you?"

"You mean you're *married?*" I needed to hear him say it.

"Yes, yes, married, exactly. Strange, when you get right down to it—one flesh and everything. Strange, but awfully nice. And you, how are you?"

He might as well have said he was a junkie, or a professional figure skater, nothing could really surprise me when it came to Loiseleur; still, it came as a shock, and I repeated stupidly, staring at the Légion d'Honneur barrette in the buttonhole of his revolting gas-blue jacket, "*Married?* To a *woman?*" I'd always assumed he was a virgin, a sixty-year-old virgin, which after all may have been the case.

"Yes, yes, a woman—they found me one." He nodded vigorously. "A student in her second year."

While I stood there, speechless, Loiseleur was intercepted by a colleague, a little old man, also eccentric in his way, but cleaner—a seventeenth-century scholar, as I remembered, a specialist in burlesques and the author of a book on Scarron. A few moments later I caught sight of Rediger in a small group at the other end of the gallery. Lately I'd been so absorbed in my preface that I hadn't thought much about Rediger. I noticed that I was truly happy to see him. He greeted me warmly, too. Now I had to call him *"Monsieur le ministre,"* I joked. "How is it?" I asked him, more seriously. "Politics, I mean. Is it really hard?"

"Yes. Everything they say is true. I thought I knew about turf wars from academia, but this is something else. Still, Ben Abbes really is an incredible guy. I'm proud to be working with him."

I thought of Tanneur and what he'd said about Augustus, that night in the Lot. The comparison seemed to interest Rediger. I'd given him something to chew on. The negotiations with Lebanon and Egypt were going well, he told me, and feelers had been put out to Libya and Syria, where Ben Abbes had rekindled old friendships with the local Muslim Brothers. Indeed, he was trying to accomplish, in one generation, through diplomacy alone, what had taken the Romans centuries. And he would add the vast territories of northern Europe, including Estonia, Scandinavia, and Ireland, without shedding a drop of blood. What's more, he had an eye for symbolism. He was about to propose that they move the European Commission to Rome and the Parliament to Athens. "Rare are the builders of empire," Rediger mused. "It is a difficult thing to hold nations together, when they're separated by religion and language, and to unite them in a common political project. Aside from the Roman Empire, only the Ottomans really managed it, on a smaller scale. Napoleon could have done it. His handling of the Israelite question was remarkable, and during his Egyptian expedition he showed that he could deal with Islam, too. Ben Abbes, yes . . . you could say he was cut from the same cloth."

I nodded energetically. He may have lost me a little with the Ottomans, but I felt at ease in the ethereal, heady atmosphere. We were two well-informed people having a polite conversation. Naturally we went on to discuss my preface; it was hard for me to detach myself from my work on Huysmans, which had preoccupied me, more or less secretly, for years. It was the entire purpose of my life, I thought with some melancholy, but I kept the thought to myself. It might sound melodramatic, but it was true. He listened closely to everything I did say, without showing the least sign of boredom. A waiter refilled our glasses.

•

"I read your book, too," I said.

"Ah . . . I'm pleased you made the time. It's not my usual thing, writing for a general audience. I hope you found it clear."

"Very clear, on the whole, though I did have a couple of questions."

We moved over to one of the windows, just far enough away to take us out of the main flow of guests, who circulated from one end of the gallery to the other. Through the casement we could see the columns and the dome of Richelieu's chapel, all bathed in cold white light. I remembered reading somewhere that his skull was preserved inside. "He was a great statesman, too, Richelieu . . . ," I said. I hadn't really thought about it, but Rediger's face lit up. "I couldn't agree more. It's amazing how much Richelieu did for France. Our kings were sometimes mediocre—that's just genetics—but their chief ministers never could be. Even now that we live in a democracy, it's odd, you see the same discrepancy. You know how highly I think of Ben Abbes— but Bayrou really is an idiot and a complete media whore. Thank God Ben Abbes has all the actual power. You're going to say I'm obsessed with Ben Abbes, but Richelieu is what made me think of him, because like Richelieu he will have done a great service to the French language. With the addition of the Arab states, the linguistic balance of Europe is going to shift toward France. Sooner or later, you'll see, the EU will make French the other working language of European institutions, along with English. But forgive me, I keep talking about politics . . . You wanted to ask about my book?"

"Well . . . ," I began, after a prolonged silence, "it's sort of embarrassing, but naturally I read the chapter on polygamy, and the thing is, I just can't see myself as a dominant male. I was thinking about it just now, when I got to the reception and saw Loiseleur. Frankly, academics . . . ?"

"I have to say, you're wrong. Natural selection is a universal principle, which applies to all living things, but it can take all sorts of forms. It exists even in the plant world, where it's a matter of access to nutritious soil, to water, to sunlight . . . Man is an animal, as we know, but he's not a prairie dog or an antelope. His dominance doesn't depend on his claws, or his teeth, or how quickly he can run. What matters is his intelligence. So—and I tell you this in all seriousness—there is nothing unnatural about classing academics among the dominant males."

He smiled again. "You know . . . That afternoon we spent at my house, we discussed metaphysics, the creation of the universe, et cetera. I'm well aware that this is not, generally speaking, what interests men; but as you were just saying, the real subjects are embarrassing to bring up. Even now, here we are discussing natural selection—we're trying to keep things on an elevated plane. Obviously, it's very hard to come out and ask, What will you pay me? How many wives do I get?"

"I already have some kind of idea about the pay."

"Well, that's basically what determines the number of wives. According to Islamic law, wives have to receive equal treatment, which imposes certain constraints in terms of housing. In your case, I think you could have three wives without too much trouble—not that anyone would force you to, of course."

•

This was food for thought, obviously, but I had one more question, and it was even more embarrassing. Before I went on, I looked around to make sure no one could hear us.

"There's something else . . . But, well, this is really awkward . . . The thing is, Islamic dress has its advantages, it's made social life so much more restful, but at the same time, it's very . . . covering, I'd say. If a person were in a situation where he had to choose, it could pose certain problems . . ."

Rediger smiled even more broadly. "There's no reason to be embarrassed! You wouldn't be a man if you didn't worry about these things . . . But let me ask you something that might sound strange: Are you sure you want to choose?"

"Uh . . . yeah. I mean, I think so."

"But isn't this an illusion? We know that men, given the chance to choose for themselves, will all make exactly the same choice. That's why most societies, especially Muslim societies, have matchmakers. It's a very important profession, reserved for women of great experience and wisdom. As women, obviously, they are allowed to see girls naked, and so they conduct a sort of evaluation, and correlate the girls' physical appearance with the social status of their future husbands. In your case, I can promise, you'd have nothing to complain about . . ."

I didn't say anything. The truth is, I was at a loss for words.

"Incidentally," Rediger went on, "if the human species has any ability to adapt, this is due entirely to the intellectual plasticity of women. Man is completely ineducable. I don't care if he's a language philosopher, a mathematician, or a twelve-tone composer, he will always, inexorably, base his reproductive choices on purely physical criteria, criteria that have gone unchanged for thousands of years. Originally, of course, women were attracted by physical advantages, just like men; but with the right education, they can be convinced that looks aren't what matters. They already find rich men attractive—and after all, getting rich tends to require above-average intelligence and cunning. To a certain degree, women can even learn to find a high erotic value in academics . . ." He gave me his most beautiful smile. For a second I thought maybe he was being ironic, but no, I don't think he was. "On the other hand, we can always just pay teachers more, which simplifies things."

He had shown me, you might say, new horizons, and I found myself wondering whether Loiseleur had used a matchmaker, but the question answered itself. Could I imagine my old colleague *hitting on* his students? In a case like his, arranged marriage was clearly the only option.

The reception was winding down, and the night was surprisingly balmy; I walked home without really thinking, in a sort of reverie. Yes, my intellectual life was finished, though I could still participate in vague colloquia and live on my savings and my pension; but I started to realize—and this was a real novelty—that life might actually have more to offer.

A few more weeks would go by, like a sort of pretend waiting period, and in those weeks the weather would grow milder day by day, and it would be spring in Paris; and then, of course, I'd call Rediger.

He'd play up his own joy, mainly out of tact, because he'd want to seem surprised, to let me feel that I was a *free agent*; his happiness would be genuine, I knew that, but I also knew that he already took my acceptance for granted. No doubt this had been true for a long time, maybe even since the afternoon I'd spent at his house in the rue des Arènes. I had made no effort to hide how impressed I was by Aïcha's physical charms, or by Malika's canapés. Muslim women were devoted and submissive, that much I could count on, it's how they were raised; they aimed to please. As for cooking, in the end I didn't really give a fuck; on that score I was less discriminating than Huysmans; but in any case, they'd received the necessary training, and you'd be hard-pressed to find one who didn't know her way around the kitchen.

•

The conversion ceremony itself would be very simple. Most likely it would take place at the Paris Mosque, since that was easiest for all involved. Given my relative importance, the dean would be there, or at least one of his senior staff. Rediger would be there, too, of course. The number of guests was entirely up to me; no doubt there would be a few ordinary worshippers as well: the mosque wouldn't close for the occasion. The idea was that I should bear witness in front of my new Muslim brothers, my equals in the sight of God.

•

That morning I would be specially allowed inside the hammam, which was ordinarily closed to men. Wrapped in a bathrobe, I would walk the long corridors with their arch-topped colonnades, their walls covered in the finest mosaics; then, in a smaller room, also covered in mosaics of great refinement, bathed in a bluish light, I would let the warm water wash over my body for a long, a very long time, until my body was purified. Then I'd get dressed in the new clothes I'd brought with me; and I would enter into the great hall of worship.

Silence would reign all around me. Images of constellations, supernovas, spiral nebulas would pass through my mind, and also images of springs, of untouched mineral deserts, of vast, nearly virgin forests. Little by little, I would penetrate the grandeur of the cosmic order. Then, in a calm voice, I would pronounce the following words, which I'd have learned phonetically: *Ašhadu an lā ilāha illā lahu,*

wa ašhadu anna muḥammadan rasūluhu: I testify that
there is no God but God, and Muhammad is the messenger
of God. And then it would be over; from then on I'd be
a Muslim.

•

The reception at the Sorbonne would be a much longer
affair. Rediger was increasingly taken up with his political
career, and had just been named foreign minister. He hadn't
much time to devote to his duties as president of the university; all the same, he'd taken it on himself to give the
speech for my induction (and I knew, I was positive, that it
would be an excellent speech, and that he'd enjoy giving it).
All my colleagues would be there—the news of my Pléiade
edition had spread in academic circles and now everybody
knew. I certainly wasn't the sort of acquaintance you'd
neglect. And everyone would be in gowns, the Saudi authorities having recently reestablished the wearing of ceremo-
nial dress.

Before I delivered my acceptance speech (by tradition,
these were very brief), I'd certainly give a last thought to
Myriam. She'd live her own life, I knew, in circumstances
much more difficult than mine. I sincerely hoped she would
have a happy life—though that struck me as unlikely.

The cocktail party would be festive, and would last into
the night.

•

A few months later there would be new classes and new
students—pretty, veiled, shy. I don't know how students find

out which teachers are famous, but they always, inevitably, did, and I didn't think things could be so different now. Each of these girls, no matter how pretty, would be happy and proud if I chose her, and would feel honored to share my bed. They would be worthy of love; and I, for my part, would come to love them.

•

Rather like my father a few years before, I'd be given another chance; and it would be the chance at a second life, with very little connection to the old one.

I would have nothing to mourn.

ACKNOWLEDGMENTS

I did not attend university, and everything I know about academic life I learned from Agathe Novak-Lechevalier, *maître de conférences* at the University of Paris X–Nanterre. If the backdrop to these inventions of mine is at all credible, it is entirely thanks to her.